Nkwala

Winner of the

Little, Brown Canadian Children's Book Award
Canadian Governor General's Award
Diploma of Merit, Hans Christian Andersen Honor List

NKWALA

by *EDITH LAMBERT SHARP*

✦ ✦ ✦ ✦ ✦ ✦ with illustrations by
William Winter, R.C.A.

LITTLE, BROWN and COMPANY
Boston, Toronto ◆━◆━◆━◆━◆

E921776

LIBRARY OF CONGRESS CATALOG CARD NO. 58-8492

Tenth Printing

Published simultaneously in Canada
by Little, Brown & Company (Canada) Limited

PRINTED IN THE UNITED STATES OF AMERICA

ACKNOWLEDGMENTS

I should like to thank:

M. W. Stirling, Director, Bureau of American Ethnology, Smithsonian Institution, for permission to use such quotes from Smithsonian publications as I desire. *Nkwala* is almost entirely based on study of Smithsonian books, even though the characters are fictional and the plot largely so. I am especially indebted to *The Salishan Tribes of the Western Plateaus* (1930) and *The Thompson Indians of British Columbia* in Volume 11 of the Memoirs of the American Museum of Natural History (April, 1900), both by James Teit, edited by Franz Boas, and published by the Smithsonian Institution.

R. N. Atkinson, Curator, Penticton Museum, for his unfailing help in the study of Indian customs and artifacts.

Lind J. LeLievre, professional guide and hunter, for infinite patience in helping me with details in the study of wildlife.

Des Haddleton, local fishing authority and radio commentator, for help in the timing of fish runs and for information on types of fish.

Bill Sutherland, hunter and amateur mineralogist, for help in wildlife detail and the identification of rock in Indian artifacts.

Jack Grigor, who organized archery in Penticton, for his help in the understanding of bow and arrow.

Charlie Armstrong, of the Penticton Indian Reservation, for the care and courtesy with which he gave me the Okanagon word for "mystery" or "monster" — nhaw-hetq.

C. P. Lyons, Provincial Department of Recreation and Conservation, a Penticton product himself, who has written the wonderfully helpful books *Trees, Shrubs and Flowers to Know in British Columbia* and *Trees, Shrubs and Flowers to Know in Washington.*

To my nephew, Terrence Charles Sharp

Nkwala

I

NKWALA was a Salish Indian boy of the Spokan tribe. The lodges of the Spokans lay east of the Ntoxetk — the Straight Water — and the people of those lodges honored the ancient laws.

Under Salish law, the night that a boy dreamed of a canoe, an arrow, or a woman, on that night his childhood lay behind him and, like the sunlight of days past, it would never return.

Ahead were days and nights of trial, when the boy went alone into the mountains to search for his guardian spirit, his song, and his name. This was as his father, his father's father, and his father's father before him, had gone. He went alone, but always and forever with him went the law.

So it was that swiftly, in the space of one dream, Nkwala's childhood was ended, toward the close of his twelfth year. Ahead were the ceremonial duties and trials when he must welcome hardship and pain, in proof of his strength and courage.

Lurking in the shadowy spots of his memory were the campfire stories of the dwarfs. These were the tales, told over the dying embers of the lodge fires, of the Little People who roamed the hills sobbing, who might make you sleepy and then steal your food.

Worse still to recall were the rumors of giants thirty feet tall, who had no upper eyelids, and therefore never slept. The giants could be recognized by the strong, unpleasant smell about them, for as much as a mile away.

True, none of these strange creatures ever harmed people, yet they were terrible to think of when one was alone with the night silence that is never silent. The night that flows into the empty spaces, and crowds close at the shoulder; the night that is breathed in and out through the nostrils, and beats on the drum of the pulse.

These were the hours when the wind talked softly with the whispering grass. Every note of the earth throbbed in the dark air in a blend of silence and a thousand tiny sounds that could pound in a boy's head like a roar if he listened too hard.

It was not good to listen too hard.

Therefore the law ordered that the boy in his ceremonies

4

must sing aloud, and pray aloud. And these prayers and these songs went up, and up, through the night and the stars to Day Dawn, the children's god, who listened, and was kind.

Many of the young people had found a name and a guardian spirit in the first four-night period they were sent out alone. But Nkwala had come back from his lonely night watches on the distant rock bluff tired and troubled.

He was puzzled as to whether he had not done everything properly. He had lit his fire that shone out high and clear to tell the whole world that he, Nkwala, had reached the time of Growing-up. He had sung the ceremonial songs, and danced the ceremonial dances, and prayed to the ancient Salish gods and to the spirits of the things about him. And still Day Dawn had not sent him his dream, nor his song, nor any special happening that would reveal his protecting guardian spirit, and give him a name.

Nkwala looked enviously at the neckbands and hair ornaments that the "grown" young people wore: ornaments made from the skin of their guardian bird or animal. He looked at the painting on their faces, which again explained the name they had found, or their guardian spirit. With a guardian spirit to help him, a Salish was brave indeed, and might do great things!

Nkwala felt unhappy, because he still wore only the plain headband of twisted cedar bark; and his hair was worn in the young boys' way, in a simple knot at his neck. About his ankles and knees were still the ceremonial deer-

5

hoof ornaments with pebbles in them that rattled as he moved. And he was still under stern ruling that allowed him to drink water only through a bone tube.

These things he would not be rid of until he had dreamed his dream, and found his guardian spirit.

So Nkwala went out for another four-day period. Then another, and another. Each time he took with him only his sleeping mat and his blanket of woven rabbit skin, his water-basket, his fire stick, and bow and arrows.

He had built himself a little sweat lodge close by a stream in which he bathed. To tire himself he went through exercises with the heavy boulders that he heated for steam in his sweat lodge. As he exercised he prayed to the spirit of sweat bathing, the Sweat-bathing Grandfather Chief, asking that he might always be strong and never be lazy, and that his life would be long and stand firm, like the strength of the rocks he carried.

If the night was bright with moonlight he practiced with his bow and arrow all night long, setting up targets for himself. If he missed the target, he ran up and down the steep hillside as fast as possible, until exhausted, to punish himself for missing.

When daylight came he steamed himself in the sweat lodge, then ran to the cold stream and bathed, rubbing himself down with fir branches and praying:

"May my body be always clean and sweet-smelling, like your sweetness, O Fir Branches. Hear me, O Spirits of the Running Water and the Fragrant Trees!"

6

So constantly he prayed and sang that it was a chant that went on and on so long as he had voice for it. He prayed to be made strong, quick, wise, brave, lucky, rich, a good hunter, a good trapper, and a good fisherman. He prayed that he might never be bewitched, or sick, or poor, or lazy, or easily tired.

And he prayed earnestly and hard for a name, and for a guardian spirit that he could call up to guard and advise him. He prayed for his own song, with which he could call that spirit. This Guardian Spirit Song he would keep throughout his manhood, and it would be to him as private a thing as his own thoughts, or his food that he put into his mouth.

But faithful though he was to every rule, Nkwala had to return to the camp again and again without a guardian spirit, and with no painting on his face. Proof of his failure he wore still the cedar headband and the deer-hoof ornaments that rattled. And his hair still was tied in the simple knot at his neck.

He began to be ashamed, for it seemed to him that he was not able to earn himself a man's name. He looked anxiously into his people's faces to see what they were thinking of him.

And they, when they saw his unhappy eyes, were sorry for him, and afraid of showing him pity, because a young boy has to develop a stout heart and must not be softened by pity. So men and women alike turned away to hide their eyes. When they turned away, Nkwala thought they were disappointed in him, and his heart was bitterly troubled.

Because he felt he could no longer stand such unhappiness alone, Nkwala went to his father, who was a man respected by the tribe and great in spirit-strength, and he said:

"All night I pray, with my heart full — not sleeping, but praying — letting my voice rise clearly that it may be pleasing to Day Dawn. I sing to the Day Dawn with a voice that the winds carry down through the sleeping valley. Surely, surely, he must hear me. And yet — he does not!"

Standing-Bear saw that the boy's face was weary, and that he had grown thinner. His heart ached for his son, and he was tempted to lend him one of his own guardian charms, as some fathers did to make things easier for their sons. But his hand stopped, even as he reached for the pouch about his neck. For there was something about the set of the boy's shoulders and the level look in the young eyes that told the father Nkwala could win this struggle alone.

So Standing-Bear put his arm about his son's shoulder, and drew him down on to the thick rush matting that covered the springy, fragrant, fir-branch bed. They leaned against the bed roll that made a back rest during the day. They watched the fire and the steam that rose from the hot rocks where berries were cooking. And they were at peace, and quiet.

8

Nkwala felt better for having told what was troubling him. Even though he had received no answer, he asked no further, for that would not have been the Salish way.

When darkness fell, Nkwala again picked up his bed roll, his water-basket, his fire drill — which was always kept in a separate pouch in his quiver — and his bow and arrows. Once more he began to leave far behind him the sweet comfort of the warm noisy nearness of people, the happy busy sounds of the camp.

But this time there was something different about his leaving.

At first, though he felt it, he did not know what it was. Then, as he took a turn in the trail, and the turn hid from him the last fire in the camp, when the great stillness that belongs to lonely mountains and to wild creatures had settled about him, he knew what the difference was about this going away.

He was growing used to it.

The path had become familiar to him. The weight of the pack that he carried was scarcely noticeable. His muscles and his nerves had become toughened by his ceremonial exercises. He was trudging along this wild and lonely trail, that he had beaten for himself, as readily as though he were a stone's throw from his family lodge.

His heart no longer jumped at every sound. True, he was wary. His eyes and ears had grown doubly keen. Through experience he now felt sure that most of the wild animals would slip away like shadows from his path. Most of them, that is, except the porcupine.

He could almost always be sure of being trailed by one curious coyote. If he cared to watch long enough and carefully enough he could see the wily animal, expert though it was at moving unseen. Its company was not unpleasant, for the very presence of the little fellow indicated that there was no cougar, grizzly, or wolverine about.

The soft, warm night air had a dry, dusty quality, and Nkwala was chewing a bit of pine gum to keep his throat from feeling dry. In all his short life he could not recall so parched a summer. The feel of it somehow made him uneasy.

After a long walk he reached the base of the big rock bluff he had chosen as his lookout and beacon sight. Tonight for the first time it seemed like a second home camp. He decided to accept the challenge of its steeper side.

The boy was agile as a mountain goat. During his periods of aloneness he had made himself familiar with every crack in the great rock surface. As he climbed, the shredded sagebrush bark in the bottom of his moccasins protected his feet from the sharp rock edges underfoot. Sometimes he pushed his pack ahead of him, sometimes he dragged it after him.

The test he set himself was that he should make no noise. The rewards of his trials were beginning to favor him. Soft-footed as the lynx, sure-footed as the bighorn, he did not once slip. This was one of the harder exercises

he had forced himself to do over and over again. He knew the way well. He had learned it with sweat running down his face and blisters rising on his hands.

He reached the proud, wind-worn top with a sense of victory, and sat down beside the ashes of his last campfire and looked around. He breathed deeply of the difference in the higher, lighter air. He heard the sounds of the night rise up to him, and he felt again that full joyfulness in his chest that mountaintops always brought to him.

His fingers searched in the cold ashes for the warmth of the cedar bark slow match he had left to nurse along a burning ember. He quickened it with shredded cedar bark and dried grass, breathed upon it till the red flames woke and set his fire to burning, shining out over the valley.

Then he sang one of his ceremonial songs, and his voice soared out like eagles' wings on the night air, and the far mountains sent him back the echo, and Nkwala felt proud to be alive.

Then, and only then, did he let himself think back to a night past — about his secret.

He was desperately ashamed of his secret.

It concerned the second night that he was out alone on his growing-up exercises. During the first night the aloneness had pressed hard, had smothered him like a black cloud. He had stayed close by his fire and kept it burning brightly for comfort. But this was not all there was to the ritual he must go through. He knew the rules. They were harsh, stern. And he, Nkwala, must follow the ancient laws if he were to gain favor with Day Dawn, the young people's god, and become a man.

Accordingly the second night he set up the triple target, three little figures of twisted and tied grass hung one above the other by bark twine from the branch of a tree. These represented three deer. The top one, with twigs for antlers, was a buck. The second figure, just a few inches below, represented a doe. The third hanging tuft of grass stood for their dappled child, the fawn.

The test was to loose four arrows at these targets by moonlight from a distance of thirty paces. Then he was to walk forward and see whether he had hit one of them. If he had failed with all four arrows, as a penalty he was to leave his camp and run for a mile. Then he was to come back and try all over again, and continue trying, and repeating the penalty, until he succeeded.

Nkwala strode out the thirty steps. He had chosen pale sun-bleached grass for the figures. He could just see them, in the moonlight that cast restless shadows dense as the thick coat of the black bear. He was a good shot, except that he had not done any night hunting.

Anxiously, he stared hard a moment to adjust his eyes to the target in the dim light. He drew back an arrow, sighted along its shaft, felt the pressure and release of the sinew cord, heard its twang muted by tufts of loon down where the sinew met the bow, heard the soft whisper of the feathered shaft — freed.

The arrow was loosed, spent, yet the target hung

in the night air as still as though it were made of stone.

He heard his breathing strangely loud. He felt dampness bead in the palms of his hands. He took off his leather hand-guard and wiped his palms against his thighs. Before this moment he had not known the cold clamp of nervousness, and so he could not judge that this was a sign that his nerves were stretched tighter than the tendon cord on his bow.

He took more time with his second arrow, fixed the nock snugly against the cord. But he felt his bow hand wavering slightly. He shifted his feet, aimed again, and fired. He was not satisfied with the way he had released the arrow.

A good hand with the bow, Nkwala always had a strangely accurate feeling telling him whether or not his arrow had found its target. Now that feeling was working against him. He chose his third arrow more carefully and released it more quickly. He thought — but he was not sure — perhaps the second figure, the doe, had quivered.

The fourth arrow, the last. The clamp of nervousness tightened. His finger felt numb. He swallowed hard against a dry throat and aimed again at the second figure. Perhaps, if it had quivered, it was a sign that the doe would bring him the most luck. He released. The feathers of the red-winged flicker cut the air, riding the shaft of the last arrow.

It was done. Four flights — spent. And that feeling about where he would find his arrows dragged dully at his heart.

He walked forward. Thirty paced-off yards of blotched

14

night light and black shadow. The grass figures hung at his eye level. A winged shaft would not pass right through the tightly bound figures of dry grass. A winged shaft would catch in the dried grass, and remain there, hanging by the bark twine. It would — if it had struck its mark.

There was no arrow hanging in any of the three targets.

When the law is learned by the heart, no ears are needed to hear its command, and the law said, "Run, for a full mile, out into the darkness, and run back, and go through the test again."

As if in a prayer for mercy, Nkwala lifted his face to the sky. But the Salish law pressed down upon him, hundreds of years old. It was trained into his brain and built into his blood stream. From such a thing one does not look for escape.

Obediently Nkwala knelt in preparation for the run, and tested his moccasin strings, snugging them firmly about his ankles. Then he built up his fire so that it would serve as a marker and guide for return, from a mile away. He carried his bow and arrow at readiness, in his hands. His quiver hung as always at his shoulder.

He looked down into the valley where the treetops were floating on dark air. He planned, when he reached the floor of the valley, to run straight north, toward the Grizzly Bear Stars, for a mile; then he would turn his back upon the guiding stars and run south, with his campfire as a return guide.

The way down the mountainside was to him a known

15

trail. But presently he found himself running in darkness over strange ground. His eyes searched for smooth running, but twice he stumbled and fell to his knees. Presently, despite unfamiliar ground and clouded moon, he gradually became more expert, and he grew a little used to the quick pat-patting of his moccasins beating out his running stride, and the rattle of the deer-hoof ornaments about his knees and ankles.

When several small dark shapes slid rapidly away from his approach, he realized that the rattling of the ornaments helped keep him safe — perhaps because the sound resembled the warning of the rattlesnake, which all animals fear.

Still, in that vast aloneness, he could hear his nervous heart pound more loudly than he could hear anything else.

With a great feeling of thankfulness he reached what he judged to be the end of the mile run. He rubbed the sweat of his hands off on the grass at his feet, and tore up handfuls of it to wipe his face. This was indeed a strange year. The grass was drier than usual, and the dust was irritating his nose. His breathing gradually quietened. He was used to long runs.

Presently he started back again, and in so doing felt a kinship for animals that turn back to their lair, for this was the homing pat-patting of his moccasins on pathless ground. He began to look for the distant flicker of his campfire. Perhaps it was because he was looking for the campfire that what happened did happen.

16

He was passing through grassland. Close by was a small stream. He could smell the marsh grasses, and the slow, sluggish water. Nighthawks and bats competed in swift dives and violent flight, hunting the insects that hung in the air above the stream — the bats silent, the birds giving their reedy, rasping cry. Low clump brushes, dimly seen, would be rich with gooseberries or currants.

Without slackening his pace, he glanced back over his shoulder to check that the Grizzly Bear Stars were straight at his back.

Then it happened.

With a strange soughing *whoof,* what he had taken to be a low bush rose up into the air straight before his face, and he collided head-on with a force that sent him spinning off his feet, and smelled hot and strong of animal.

The careful balance in which he was holding his nerves snapped. He had no recollection later, of striking the ground — it was marsh grass in his clothing that told him he had fallen. He did not know that he rose again with the speed of a coiled rattler and ran like a mad thing, with his breath sucking in and out of his chest with loud noises, and his mind blanked out in terror.

He ran without sense of direction. Nkwala was in complete hysteria. He could not have stopped himself running if he had tried. He did not know when he left the grassy flat and tore crazily over a dry hillside and through cactus that buried hooked spikes in his ankles and legs. Nor did he know the moment that exhaustion and faintness overcame

him and he pitched forward and lay unconscious, face down.

The Cluster Stars that tell off the hours of darkness moved farther toward the place of their going down. A low wind swept the ground, as though the night were drawing a deep breath, and there were dry rustlings and whispers in the grass about Nkwala. Painfully he struggled back to consciouness.

His head ached. The collision on the grass flats had made his nose bleed. Blood was drying on his face and chest. Even his clenched hands ached, but as he moved them he was grateful for the feel of his bow. He sat up, suddenly fearful, and groped for his quiver. It, too, was there, with the arrows. So much to the good.

His eyes searched the shadows of the near hillside for any animal that might have decided to creep up on him as he lay fallen. As he turned about, he realized that his whole body was stiff.

Then, with the full return of consciousness, came the agony of the pain in his legs from the cactus spikes.

Beads of sweat were standing out on his face before he had pulled the last burning barb from his flesh, and his legs were as blood-covered as were his face and chest.

He felt the throb of pain through his whole body, and the aching need to get back to where he could rest. He walked to the crest of a knoll and sighted his mountaintop with its glimmer of firelight, and set out for it at a limping trot.

Reaching his rock bluff he went first to the stream at its base, and washed the blood from his face, and held his legs in the cool water till the burn from the cactus poison was numbed. With his fingers he dug under the sedges, the grasslike hollow-stemmed plants, for smooth wet mud which he plastered over his legs, and the unfailing good of the earth went to work drawing out the poison, soothing and healing.

These things done, he climbed to his mountaintop and made his fire blaze high. His heart took comfort while he watched the flames, which were beautiful to him at that moment. Then he fell on his bed roll, and slept.

That night was the night of Nkwala's secret, which he told no one, for shame.

The sun was high when he woke. He rolled over, and let the warmth sink into him. And he began to think.

Nothing had really hurt him, except his own fear.

He had been running into the wind, and what he had collided with on the grasslands was probably a startled deer, or elk, that rose to its feet and rushed off, as frightened as he.

And he, Nkwala, had let fear pick him up and shake him as a dog shakes a mole or a gopher. He had been blinded and crazed by fear. Unconscious, he had lain like live bait on a hillside.

That was the way of death to the hunter. That was the trap of no return, to the lone traveler. Nkwala knew it now.

Indeed, had not his own spirit left his body while he lay with his face buried in the earth. He shivered.

"I have learned, by going," Nkwala whispered to the ashes of his fire. "My spirit walked the White Trail in the sky. But it has returned to me, stronger than before.

"And never again will I, Nkwala, let fear run within me wild and unchecked. Though I may feel fear, yet will I hold it as a running dog is held by the halter rope."

He was growing excited. He leaped to his feet and held his clenched fists up to the sky, shouting the vow that formed on his lips, the vow that was to live with him during all the days of his whole life:

"So long as Nkwala lives, Fear will never again have its way with him — *never!*"

The hills sent the echo back in waves of sound on the warm sunny air:

"Never! . . . Never! . . . Never!"

He was trembling with the passion of his promise, and the sudden realization that through pain he had gained in wisdom. He could feel the growth that the terrible night had brought to him. So he lifted his face again to the god of the young people, and he cried loudly:

"Be it known to you, O Day Dawn, that Nkwala is no longer a child!"

And the hills called back their answer:

"Child! . . . Child! . . . Child!"

But though Day Dawn and the echoes heard, still was no sign sent to Nkwala; and the waiting was long.

Only the steady beating of a crow's caw followed the slow dying of the echo. Nkwala realized that he was hungry, and dug into his bed roll for some serviceberry cake. Then he began the serious job of washing the blood off his clothes, and putting fresh mud pack on his legs, so that his people would not see the barb wounds, when he got back, and thus guess what had happened.

The secret of that night Nkwala kept locked behind his lips and told no one. Now, many nights later, he was able to sit easily by his fire and enjoy his singing to Day Dawn.

The three little grass figures hanging by bark twine from the branch had been riddled by arrows riding the night shadows. Riddled and worn out and replaced, too many times to count. Often all four of his arrows found their target by moonlight, and his confidence in his marksmanship was high. Still he practiced endlessly.

He still exercised, running with heavy rocks, then hurling them as far as he could, often over a cliff, when he listened to their slow rolling thunder in a deep-throated canyon. Then the songbirds darted upward on startled wings, and the squirrels came out to investigate and remained to scold. He went for long, unbroken runs, so that like the coyote he knew every hillock, meadow, and bluff of what he had taken as his territory. He knew where the hare ran for cover, and where the deer came to drink. He knew the salt licks where the great bucks came at daybreak, and the berry plots where the black bear grew fat.

And he marked that these signs grew less and less as the country grew drier and drier.

He sweat-bathed every day, and plunged several times a day into the pool in the bed of the cold stream. And he still prayed constantly for his guardian spirit, but none was sent to him.

He was afraid that his people were laughing at him, saying, "His voice is weak, the Day Dawn cannot hear him!"

But they were not, for they knew the laws of the growing-up ceremonies better than he. And they were saying one to another, "Nkwala's growing-up exercises go into a long time of many days. He will be a remarkable man."

Nkwala did know that if his ceremonial exercises ran on into many moons and other summers, he would be expected to become a shaman. This he did not want, as he had no yearning for power over his people, nor did he like the solitary life of the shaman. He loved the company of his people. He wanted to be with them, one of them, even as now on this night he knew loneliness.

But it was not his absence from his people at this moment of silent, heat-throbbing drakness that was making him uneasy.

For two nights past he had missed the soundless shadowing of his shy little follower, the coyote. The animal had been accepting food of his killing. Nkwala would pick off fat groundhogs as they sunned themselves on a rock near their holes, and leave them for the coyote. The wild creature ate his meal so cleanly that Nkwala knew there was

23

no easy hunting for him in the near hills, either by day or by night, for the coyote hunts both in daylight and in darkness.

The boy's songs to Day Dawn usually brought forth an answering volley of cries from the coyote. But now Nkwala's song was ended, and there was only silence. Great forest-toned, drifting waves of silence.

Suddenly lonely, Nkwala tipped back his head and gave the call of the coyote. There was no response. This was most strange.

Nkwala stepped to the edge of his high camp ground, filled his chest with air, and gave a call that was entirely his own. He had been practicing, to find a sound that the echoes would carry farthest, and had developed something like a yodel.

He listened while the echoes picked up the bell-like tones and carried them on, and on, and on. If his wild pet were in the near hills at all, it would answer to that.

There was no wilderness reply. Only the echoes, dying. The coyote had left. He had changed his hunting grounds.

Now it is taught to every Salish, in order that he may live, that nothing happens without a reason and a cause. And it is also taught, in order that he may live, that the reason and the cause mark the trail that the Salish must follow in his mind.

Therefore uneasiness prickled over Nkwala's skin like a cold breeze. But the hot air was scarcely stirring, the trees were barely murmuring their songs — they that could shake their heads and roar like a waterfall when the wind was high!

The earth, though it had lain for hours in the darkness, threw back a heat like the cooking-stones in a lodge fire.

Nkwala rubbed the sweat off his forehead and rolled the pine gum around in his dry mouth.

Suddenly it was as though the wilderness that he had learned to know so well put a warning hand on his shoulder and said, "The night birds, Nkwala, listen for the night birds."

He listened. This night had its sounds, but these were not the full sounds of its busy, normal life. Too much silence. His ears were trained to sounds that should be there, but were not.

When his instincts commanded him, he acted swiftly. Nkwala stooped, rolled and tied his blankets. He emptied his water-basket on his campfire, and saw how fiercely the hot flames fought to live in the dry air. He threw sand over the warm ashes and stamped it down until the last ember was smothered and black. Then he shouldered his blanket roll and water-basket and set out at a swift trot for his home camp and his people.

Nkwala's father was in the gathering of men sitting in late conference about the council fire when the boy stepped out of the shadows.

Standing-Bear gave his son a long look, that understood much.

"How so, boy?" said one of the old men whose age en-

titled him to ask any question he wished. "You are returned so soon?"

Nkwala answered unsmiling, "The coyote is wise. Should Nkwala be less wise?"

The men were grave: "What of the east hills, Nkwala?"

Then Nkwala stepped forward and gave his report like a scout, for it is the right of every Salish male to be heard in council, so long as he has something to say.

"The grass on the east hills is tinder under the fire stick. The hare has forsaken the shadow of the sagebrush, and the rabbit does not graze in the flatlands. The home of the beaver crumbles in the hot sun, for the stream has become small. The beaver people have left. They are not in their home."

After a moment he added, "And the coyote has left."

The men waited for him to sit down, to indicate that he had finished speaking. But Nkwala looked into their faces, one after the other, and finally he said, "My coyote. If you see him, do not kill him."

The chief, Running-Elk, rubbed his hand across his lips to hide a smile. He asked, "But how will we know your coyote, Nkwala?"

The boy replied, "He follows close, and he has a great curiosity."

This time the chief could not hide his smile. "You have been feeding him, Nkwala?"

Nkwala nodded, suddenly shy, and the men all burst out laughing. They patted his shoulder and rubbed his head, till he rocked on his heels and his headband was askew, but one and all they said to him, "The coyote does not forget, Nkwala. He will bring you luck. Wait and you will see."

II

NKWALA's people were breaking camp from the lake shore that had known the sound of their voices and the smoke of their fires since long before he was wrapped in fawn skin and placed in a bark basket.

The country was so dry that the terror of forest fires hastened their leaving. No one was allowed to carry fire, and only indoor lodge fires were permitted.

The women grumbled about the way they had to reach into their stored food and caches during these many days past while the drought grew worse and the hunting was poor. The next minute they grumbled about the vast amount of baskets, mats, stored food, and clothing that they had to leave behind.

But no one scolded them, or said, "Why do you grumble so?" Because the women's real trouble was dread of the journey, and fear of how they might be received in a strange country.

Stripped to moccasins and breechcloths, the men worked in the panting heat, selecting what was to be carried, allotting so much to each, according to his or her strength.

What was left they made into caches — some on platforms in the tree branches, wrapped in tule mats and tied down with hemp rope and leather thongs. Most of the food they cached in stone and clay-lined holes in the ground. Even their cooking ovens they had to use for storage, for the Spokans were a hard-working, hard-hunting tribe, and their wealth was considered great by all who had heard of them.

When their work was done, their chief, Running-Elk, gave final orders. Then they slept. The next morning they rose before day break. Their meal was light. Their burdens were heavy. Their hearts, too, were heavy. There had been no migration in the memory of any of their young people. They had stayed in one place, worked hard, and prospered.

Now the drought was driving them away. The great heat had panted and shimmered on the hills and over the camass meadows and the berry fields, day after breathless day.

Since the warm moon of the spring and the gathering of nest eggs and the birth of the fawn, the earth had

waited for the cool touch of rain. In vain the people had sung their rain songs. In vain their shaman had put on his rain mask and whirled, leaped, and stamped through his rain dance. Still the cloudless heat pressed down upon them. Now, sad in their hearts, they were leaving their sun-parched home.

Swiftly the people gathered in the morning dusk, shadows moving silently out of the shadows. Soft-voiced shadows, heavy and lumpy with their burdens, speaking in hushed tones, as though someone had died. Not even the barking of a dog was heard, for they had sent their dogs south with a few of their band when the drought began, as they had been concerned about feeding them.

Four scouts had gone on ahead, fanning out over their advancing trail, to warn and to guide. Two scouts hung back, to guard the people against attack from the rear. The children and women were placed in the center of the march, the men on the outside. Every man was armed, even to small knives tucked into leggings, sashes, and sleeves. Peaceful though they were, they had not forgotten the ways of war, and in the unknown country lurks the unknown.

At a word from the chief, the Spokan people began their long trek. Nkwala watched their moccasins. He could not takes his eyes away from all those obediently moving feet.

North by northwest they were treading, already striking a pace they could hold for days.

How far would his people go? When might they return

32

to their lodges and their lake shore? He looked back upon their empty camp.

The lodge fires that had burned unceasingly, day and night for years, burned no more. The deep, dark-shining lake, daily shrinking into its shores, already looked deserted. Water-washed branches that had lain hidden under water in the full lake now stood upthrust, bleached and white in the hot air, as though the lake were giving up the skeletons of its dead.

Suddenly Nkwala ducked out from under the tumpline that balanced his pack upon his shoulders, set the burden down, and ran back to the lonely lake. He picked up a smooth stone from the shore, breathed upon it, and skipped it onto the still water.

He spoke. His voice carried strangely, as though already the place were haunted by ghosts with echo voices:

"Be it known to you, O Lake, that Nkwala and his people will return to you. Swell and grow great again, and remember us, your people, for we will come back. Hear, O Lake! Listen and remember, for this is my promise."

Softly in its silence the lake gave back one echoed word:

" . . . *Promise!* . . ."

Then Nkwala ran back, picked up his burden, and stepped into the moving column of his people. His father's watchful eye was upon him.

After that began a pattern of days that were full of footsteps. Walk . . . walk . . . walk. The steps were not rapid, but they were steady, like the pulse in Nkwala's wrist. So steady that the miles flowed under the Salish moccasins.

They moved westward, toward the mountains that stand against the sea mists, and northerly, toward the country of the blue spruce and the big, heavy-antlered moose.

Each night they put fresh moss or shredded bark into their moccasins. Each day it was pressed flat under the soles of their patient feet.

Each night under safety of darkness they drew in beside the stream they were following, and bathed, and drank and ate, and rested, and said their prayers, and slept; while not all the bird and animal cries about them were uttered by birds and animals, but every so often by their scouts.

Nkwala lay awake, listening.

"Our upstream scout would not trick the ears of the coyote," he whispered into the dark, and the slow smoke of a bark smudge.

His father rolled on one naked shoulder and lifted himself to his elbow.

"And does this critic — my son — feel that *his* throat could deceive both the scout and the coyote?"

"He who taught me does better," replied Nkwala quickly — then, wisely, waited for his father to speak, for the young do not take issue with their elders.

And the father knew himself checked, because it was he who had taught Nkwala the cry of the coyote. He smiled, and reached out and tugged gently at the knot of thick hair at his son's neck.

"And has the woman, my wife, given birth to a little spotted sandpiper, that he must swim for himself while he is still wet from the shell?"

Nkwala heard his mother's soft laugh, the first since they had left their home camp. The boy rolled over onto his father's arm and rubbed his cheek against it, taking comfort against the strangeness of his surroundings. So lying, he fell asleep.

After a time the woman spoke:

"There is a mark upon our son. His childhood itches him like a goatskin robe!"

"The mighty pine lies curled in the small naked seed," said her husband, "and who can say how it thrusts against its prison? But my woman speaks truth. Perhaps Day Dawn, the children's god, understands this small one who would outleap his years."

The night flowed over the camp like a river of cool hours, till the flare along the ridges turned into daylight, and the red flush of the dawn told of the heat that would follow when the sun rode high.

While the birds were still squabbling over their morning feeding grounds, the party broke camp and made swiftly for the shelter of the big timber at the mountain's base, their water-baskets fresh, heavy, and cold. A warmer burden were the young children, still limp, silent, and big-eyed with sleep. After a while they would run. But these were strange hours for the very young.

Now the pattern of the valley and their need to reach water each night held them on a northerly course. By day, the weight of their packs pressed the tumplines hard into their foreheads, and the sweat beaded heavily above their lips. By night, the Grizzly Bear Stars showed upon their forward trail before the march was stopped.

Then the scouts who had been on duty came in to eat and sleep while others took their places, and the men discussed the signs that had been seen during the day. Nkwala's hemp headband with its three hawk feathers was a familiar sight in the evening gathering, where the boy edged and eased himself tightly into the center of the group, so that he might hear all that was being said.

"Nkwala is like his coyote," said one of the men, "he has a great curiosity!" The men all laughed, and laughter was so rare during this march that Nkwala laughed too, and trembled with delight that the full council of men should recognize him.

Then the last of the change of scouts strode into camp and his face was dark, like a cloud that warns of a storm.

"Ho!" he exclaimed. "This is no good thing that I have found."

A path opened for him as he walked up to Running-Elk, the chief. He held out the thing that was in his hand. It was nothing more than a half-burned piece of bark from the yellow pine. But the people knew, and the word passed back to those who could not see:

"Enemy firewood!"

Choice of warring or marauding parties, the bark of the yellow pine makes but a small smoke, and its heat dies quickly, making it difficult to tell how long ago the fire has been lighted.

The chief examined the charred bark. "The sand beneath it," he said, "was it warm?" The scout shrugged helplessly. "Since the sun rose high and our shadows shortened, all has been heat. The touch of the hot rocks, the breath of the hot wind, and the hot pitch bubbling in the bark of the living trees. How could I tell?"

"Where found you the enemy firewood?"

"On a bluff overlooking a path — like an ambush over a trail!"

"You spoke truth. This is no good thing."

And Running-Elk turned to the chief of the march, and ordered the scouts to be doubled in number. Then he spoke to his people.

"Evil walks the floor of this valley, and fear is its shadow. Man hunts for man when the yellow pine bark burns, and no man stops to reason when the arrow has left the bow.

"We come in peace, asking only to live till the great heat leaves our own land — but we may yet pay the price for blood that is not of our spilling.

"Each man digs in his own ground. Therefore listen,

37

while the chief of the march will speak of the things concerning the march."

The man who had been chosen chief and adviser of the long trek stepped forward, for every Salish knows the value of a little open ground when he wishes to command the attention of his people.

"We build no beds by the stream tonight! Fill your water-baskets with haste, for like the wary buck, we drink and take cover. Keep the children close, and move shoulder to shoulder. Sleep in your outer garments, and with your moccasins upon your feet. Keep your weapons at your side. All these things we shall do until we reach safety."

Nkwala tugged at the fringe of his father's tunic; "Where is this place called 'safety'?"

His father handed him a water-basket to fill.

"The cougar pulls down the deer, and the coyote waits for the marmot. The otter lifts the fish from the stream, and man hunts man. This 'safety' place I have not found. Does my son's heart yearn for such a place?"

"Nkwala is one with his people. Where they walk, there too are his footsteps."

They moved back into the shelter of the big trees at the mountain's base. The people lay down to sleep. A baby cried, and its mother spoke, comforting it. All sound in the patch of forest was muffled, faint, smothered in the heavy pine and fir branches, and absorbed by the years and years and years of fallen needles, brown, weather-polished, and slippery.

38

Here and there was the firefly flicker of a jade pipe, its owner drawing comfort through the maplewood stem from the smoke of his wild tobacco mixed with kinnikinnick.

Nkwala's eyes did not want to close. A catbird mewed plaintively overhead. A mourning dove answered with its endless sadness. They were unwise. The five-foot span of the great gray owl's wingspread moved like a shadow among the branches. A pine cone fell. A song was ended.

"This 'safety' place," his father had said, "I have not found."

A man rose from his rest and went and leaned against a great boulder, apart from the sleepers. His eyes looked northward, along tomorrow's trail. He was Running-Elk, their chief.

Nkwala pushed aside his robe, and followed on silent feet. He stood back, respectfully, until the man recognized him.

"And has Nkwala such long thoughts that he must stay awake to keep pace with them?"

"This 'safety' place — " Nkwala began, but the chief shook his head. After a while he began to speak, but carefully, and with thought, for the instruction of the young is a serious matter.

"In all the days of travel that a man can make, no trail leads to 'safety.' All the safety Nkwala will ever find, he will find . . . within himself. It lies . . . it lies in knowing what thing to do, and in doing that thing.

"Sometimes — " the man turned his eyes to the north as

39

though he would read its thoughts — "sometimes the trail is faint indeed. But it is in my mind tonight that up there someone has struck, and someone mourns, and every man's hand is upon his knife."

For much longer than Nkwala's few years, the Spokan people had been too serious and industrious to make war, and too dangerous for any to dare attack them. But the blood in his veins was the blood of Salish warriors who had leaped to the beat of the war drum, and now this blood was thudding like a drum in his head.

Running-Elk studied the excited gleam in the young eyes, and frowned heavily.

"Are hot thoughts wise thoughts — are hot words wise words?"

Nkwala shook his head mutely, ashamed of his excitement, and shaken by these surging changes sweeping through him like a great force.

"I am many people this night," he thought, "and I cannot understand all these people that I am."

He felt the desperate earnestness in Running-Elk's voice as the grave tones concluded, "Under yonder sky to the north we shall meet those we do not know, *and no blood must flow!*"

The words sank deep, and deep, into Nkwala's memory.

Troubled, he lifted his face as if in prayer to Day Dawn; for there, far up and high, where walked the everlasting winds, were the answers to questions that called within his mind — called without answer.

So it was that while his mind searched, his eyes were lifted to the Grizzly Bear Stars, hanging in the north, followed eternally by the three Hunter Stars, and crossed and zigzagged by the hungry flight of a nighthawk crying, "Pee-yah, pee-yah!"

Nkwala lifted his arm. "The Bear!" he cried, pointing. He felt excitement chill his skin despite the night's sullen heat. "The Grizzly Bear, my chief, it lowers its head to drink. Surely, surely it sees where the rain clouds gather!"

Running-Elk lifted his head and tested the scents of the air like a great gray wolf.

"For two nights past the Bear of the Sky has stooped, but little. Only a little. And the air," he shook his head, "this air is dry. It has no smell of rain."

Nkwala's spirits sank again. Man and boy, they leaned in silence against the stone and listened to the high, thin, dry sorrow of the wind — a weak, complaining wind that parched their skins but made no motion in its passing.

The only moving thing about them was the nighthawk feeding on the wing, flashing and diving in untiring speed, crying its buzzing, beetle-like rasp, "Pee-yah, pee-yah!"

Suddenly the tassled top of a slim yellow pine began to sway. Alone in all the stillness it moved. Then a lone hemlock, lover of shadow and moisture, swung its heavy, fragrant arms, and was still.

Quick touches of unexpected motion rippled here and there like feathered arrows of wind loosed without reason.

41

There was a new lightness to breathe. Nkwala's nostrils found it, and his lungs sucked it in hungrily. He lifted his arms into it. His whole body told him that things were happening in the air. He looked at Running-Elk.

Under its dust of travel the chief's face relaxed into a smile.

"Messengers," he said, indicating the bits of wind that tugged and pulled lightly here and there and slipped on. "They say that where they go, in a little time the big wind will come . . . Listen!"

The low notes of the ground winds were just beginning. They heard them coming closer, sweeping over the valley floor like a soft-footed army, bringing with them the sweet, longed-for smell of rain.

"The drums of the sky will beat a loud song when this rain falls!" said Running-Elk.

Two bats left their sluggish perch and joined the nighthawk in the wild freedom of starlit flight. Nkwala's spirits soared to join them.

Somewhere on the eastern side of the valley a coyote lifted his nose to the new winds and gave voice. That was the signal, and silence followed it.

"Listen with your heart, Nkwala." The man's voice was low. "Listen with your heart, and you will hear the quiet feet of our coyote brothers moving toward their singing posts."

Then the two were still. But Nkwala's heart was not still. It leaped with the flight of the nighthawk's wings, and climbed to the crests of the lonely lookouts with the gathering coyotes.

Presently the singing began, and the whole night rocked with the sound — wild, joyous, and full-throated.

"Sing, little coyote brothers," said the Spokan chief softly, "call and shout in gladness, for the long dry time is ending."

By morning the tall trees roared and tossed in storm, and the dark clouds were herded in to crowd the sky. Thunder started far south and sent its echoes, then marched north along the mountain ridges beating out its deep rolling crashes till it spilled over in terrible sounds that were laced together with flashing needles of lightning.

A tall pine tree was struck, and the people, huddled under their robes, turned their eyes away from it, and from the injured tree's great white wound from tip to root, and the smoke that began to smolder at its base — for lightning fire is evil fire, and the man who uses it will become sick. The Salish uses only the fire that is made and fed by Salish hands.

At last, though suddenly, the storm was ended, with only muttering, angry thunder, growling as it moved on still farther north; and large, heavy raindrops began to fall, making pitted black spots in the gray dust.

The people laughed like children, and cupped their hands to catch the rain. They sang their rain song, which was a prayer of thanks. Sifting down through the air that was filled with the sound of their voices, the raindrops changed to a torrent that sank into the ground, and the green things started to drink deep.

Then the littler young ones shrieked and capered and danced in the white flash of the driving rain. Thirsty, they lifted openmouthed faces to the sky like hungry nestlings that hear the rustling return of the mother bird.

Nkwala was too old for such display, but his heart was happy. He heard his father say, "It is long since we have heard the drum of the beating rain. Now it drums upon strange ground. Yet it falls, sweet as the touch of honey upon our lips, and we are glad."

The people, who had been tense and quiet during the long hard trek, relaxed a little, and after the manner of those whose spirits have risen they talked more freely of the things that lay dark and troubling in their minds.

"Cool weather makes cooler judgment," said a man whose summers were many. "Now it may be that those we meet will listen to the talk that our chief will wish to make to them."

"If we reach the waters of Soiyus without the flat-headed arrows flying . . . " said another.

Nkwala was listening. "Soiyus meant "Gathered To-gether" or "Meeting Place"; and the flat-headed arrow was usually dipped in poison, and was shot with the head lying flat so that it could better pass between a man's ribs. It was the war arrow.

"I weary of traveling like a hunted rabbit!" said a young

man sharply. His fingers toyed with the keen edge of a war knife.

The older man turned to him slowly, deliberately, but his words had a sharper cut than the edge of the knife. He pointed toward the women and children. "Does the young man need to be reminded that he is not traveling alone?"

The young man flushed, but his punishment was not yet over.

"And does not the flute that he carries about his neck teach him something about a man's care for his people?"

Those who heard smiled, for it was well known that the thin, sweet music that was often heard as they drifted off to sleep came from the flute hanging upon the young man's broad chest, and that, after the manner of his people, he serenaded the shy, brown-skinned beauty of his choice.

"My words were rash," said the young man. "Do not tell the maiden or the people of her lodge that my words were rash."

"It is forgotten," replied the older man, and the others nodded and echoed, "It is forgotten."

"We must be patient each one with the other, and must slow to anger with the stranger," said one.

"So that when the time comes, our chief may have a little time to talk and to claim our ancient right," said another.

"My people chatter like blackbirds in swamp tules after this rain," thought Nkwala, "and this thing of which they talk, Nkwala does not know." Therefore he searched the groups for the hawk feather that stood upright in his father's headband. No feather rode higher or more proudly in Spokan headdress. And so his father felt the familiar tug on the buckskin fringe of his tunic, and turned to face his young son, who was forever full of questions.

"This 'time for talk' which shall be in the words of our chief and spoken to strangers — " began Nkwala, with the words tumbling from him — "this 'first talking' that will speak of a 'right' — "

Standing-Bear looked at his son for a silent moment, and shook his head with some wonderment.

"The rains have fallen," he said, "and the little children have danced in the falling. The older children even now float toy canoes in the pools that the storm has left. But Nkwala is not among them."

"But — but — " said Nkwala, and his eyes filled with tears in the fear that his father was not pleased with him. He could neither understand nor explain that day after day, alone, in his growing-up ceremonies, he had become estranged from the other children; and that moon after moon of aloneness had forced him toward the thoughts of an older person. And that he bore indeed, but hidden and upon his spirit, that mark of difference of which Bright-Star, his mother, had spoken.

"There is a mark upon our son," she had said. "His childhood itches him like a goatskin robe!"

The father steered Nkwala out of the crowd with a hand upon his shoulder, and sat down to answer his questions.

"My son, when we left behind us the Ntoxetk, which was growing small under the wrath of the hot sun, the bands of the neighboring country, the Wenatchi and the Kalispel — whom we know and whom we greet upon the hunters' trail with friendliness — these also we left behind.

"Now we move among strangers, and the path under our feet is a troubled path, for the signs read that other strangers have moved upon these paths ahead of our coming.

"We walk upon a trail that others have fouled and made treacherous. They have come with the war arrow and the war knife, and they have struck while they themselves were hidden.

"We come with the hemp twine, and with dressed skins, and with the camas root, to trade. But the fire of hatred is scorching this valley, and the people's minds are hot from its burn. Therefore our chief must have a little time to speak the cooling words of friendliness, *before* . . ." Standing-Bear paused . . . "*before* Spokan blood flows. For no man spills the blood of a Spokan but he pays the price."

There was a long silence, during which Nkwala shivered as though the day were cold.

"There is more evil to this thing than I have spoken," said the father. "But Nkwala my son has asked, and therefore I speak."

The boy's eyes did not move from his father's face.

"If this blood flows — " Standing-Bear lifted his gaze

to the tallest mountain on the horizon, as the Salish do when praying — "if this blood flows between Okanagon and Spokan, the Great Spirit will be angered, and will turn his face from his children, for the man who strikes — *spills his own blood!*"

Standing-Bear turned and looked at his son, who had neither moved nor spoken, though his eyes had widened at these words.

"This is the 'right' of which you have heard. Our blood right. Our blood right to the hunting grounds and the root-digging grounds of the Okanagons, as they have in turn blood right to ours. For in days past beyond counting — it may be when the rocks themselves were young — the Okanagon and the Spokan were one, of a name called the 'Flathead Tribe.'

"This thing Amotqen, the Great Spirit, knows, and if blood should spill between us he will be angered, and without his kindness his children perish."

And now Nkwala did a thing which in the eyes of his father was very strange. For having been told these grave and serious things, he suddenly became gay and carefree, as indeed the whole world seemed to be; for the air was filled with sweet smells and birdsong, and in their forest grove the pine branches sent their fragrance out over the cones that had dropped thickly upon the ground during the storm.

Nkwala eyed the shouting pine-cone battle that was going on between two boys of his own age. Then he gathered his own pine cones and crept stealthily toward the other two in surprise attack.

A squirrel chittered angrily overhead. His objections were violent, as he had an interest of his own in the sweet, nut-flavored seeds of the fallen pine cones.

Standing-Bear stared after his son with a puzzled look in his eyes. Then he turned back to help his wife pack the deer bladders of shredded venison and of mixed pounded roots, serviceberry, and deer fat into the food bags. He checked on his and his families' footgear. No broken moccasin laces could be risked, as the chief of the march had asked them to make faster time in the more open country ahead.

After a moment Nkwala's mother said, "My husband is silent."

"For this I am glad," replied Standing-Bear, indicating the mock battle that was filling the air with pine cones, "that my son is a child again. But . . ." and he tried to explain to his wife how Nkwala had asked him the most serious questions. And because he had asked, he was told these grave matters, whereupon he had at once become carefree.

The woman gave him her shy smile.

"My husband looks into a clear pool that gives him back his own reflection, for the son is like the father. And I, the woman, have loved both, therefore this is what I see:

"The men of the council spoke truth when they said that

Nkwala was like his coyote, with a great curiosity. The coyote wants to know all. He will circle back to study his enemy. And he will follow and watch and listen, and will himself stay hidden, in order that he may know all.

"So it is with Nkwala. And when his mind knows that which it did not know, then he makes peace with his mind, and is happy."

Their talk was interrupted. The scouts who had ranged out ahead of them during the storm came back with their reports, the embroidered fringes of their outer robes still soggy and heavy with rain.

"I have seen the family markings in these people's berry grounds," said one, "and the berries have been eaten only by the birds, and by the bears."

"I have walked across the root-digging grounds of these people," said another, "and the digging that was done in their ground is not of this season."

Running-Elk turned to his people and raised his voice so that all might hear:

"You have heard these words, which are not good," he said. "The trail under our feet runs north, but tread it softly, each one of you, for the north is unhappy. And what benefits a chief who counts his dead when the cold moon closes in and the harvests are not gathered? Move carefully and be slow to anger when the stranger is met. These are my words to you."

Standing-Bear felt his son's shoulder pressing against his arm, for true to his habit Nkwala had squirmed his way into the center of the council, so that he might not miss anything that was being said. The father gave his usual gentle tug to his son's hair knot, and the boy leaned back against him for a moment.

After that came again the weight of the pack, the pressure of the tumpline against the forehead, and the lengthened stride for the moccasin. Pemmican and water made quick meals, and the people slept only during the darkest hours, traveling in the dusk of night and morning. The burdens had to be taken from the elder ones, and the little ones often had to be carried.

During the march, as he often did, Nkwala was studying the sky. The high wind was playing joyfully with the clouds that the storm had left behind.

It smoothed out vast, breathlessly white valley floors, and piled up great gleaming mountains. Then it tore them up into surf and foam and spilled sunlight over them and through them. Here was the beauty of the sky for which the Spokan heart had longed during the dry days of the glaring heat. Not even their sense of danger could blind them to the glory that was shifting and spreading before them.

Nkwala was matching his stride to his mother's.

"Nkwala's heart yearns to follow such a trail," whispered the boy, indicating high overhead a shining, cloud-white path with sunshine beckoning at its end.

Nkwala's mother was a pretty woman, who wound seashells and ermine skins in her black hair, and saw beauty in everything her soft brown eyes beheld.

"And what would my son hunt?" she replied, for this "Hunting in the Sky" was an old and secret game between them.

"Sunbeams!" replied Nkwala. "Sunbeams with the velvet of the morning on their antlers. With magic bow and arrow, I, Nkwala, would track them down the rainbow, and through the far trails of the sky, and catch them as they stooped to drink at the streams of the Eternal Winds!"

Their game of pretend was halted by a signal from a scout on the eastern side of the valley. For while the people with their burdens traveled the easy, level ground, the scouts moved ahead on the mountains, which gave them full view of the flat land for miles.

The chief of the march replied to the scout's signal for attention, whereupon he received the signs of "Lake," "Good," and "Come out" or "Come on." Then the sharp, daylight, yipping call of the coyote was heard faintly from the hills around them. This was the "All Clear" from their other scouts, to the north, south, east, and west.

So it was that with an easy heart the Spokans topped a slight rise and got their first glimpse of the full, clean little lakes and the miles of good clean grass of "Soiyus," the "Gathered Together" or "Meeting Place."

This great hollow of gold and drowsy heat lent itself to peaceful talk and careful consideration among Indian bands, and the Spokans had counted on meeting some

53

traveling or fishing or trading groups here, and spreading the word that their coming was in peace and with things to trade.

But the sole ruler of these miles of sleepy silence was a great seven-pronged elk, fat with good pasture and fresh water, who studied them for a startled moment with an expression that said, "*They* weren't here a moment ago!" Then as he was downwind and caught their scent, he swung his proud head and made off, while a loon, in its shallow marshy bay, voiced its crazy, quivering "*Ha-ha-ha-ha-ha!*"

And the Spokan scouts and hunters, hungry though they were for red meat, after traveling many days on dried foods, stared after the royal elk, but murmured, "Peace, Little Brother. The Spokans do not hunt this day."

Safe in their smallness, the yellow warblers moved in quick restlessness through the silverleaf sand-bar willow till its lithe branches dripped the golden notes of birdsong.

A porcupine waddled across the Spokan path, impudent in its ignorance that its quills made excellent embroidery, and that its flesh was sweet and tender.

Shoveler and mallard ducks moved nervously toward the far ends of the lakes, but the black coot, unconcerned, continued its noise and fussing and splashing, while the killdeer ran up and down the wet sand, crying its own name.

But not any of this untouched plenty was wholly pleasing in the eyes of Running-Elk, the Spokan chief. He flung down his pack and his hand rubbed at the deep imprint of

54

the tumpline on his forehead. It had no effect on the gathering frown that was stirring up the darkness of anger and anxiety in his eyes.

"Where," he demanded loudly, "are the Salish?" and the people stared at him, saying nothing, while the echo of his voice struck the granite hillside, and a great-horned mountain ram gathered his sharp pointed hoofs under him and leaped from rock to rock till one loosened beneath his springing thrust and rolled into the valley, its echoes joining those of the voice that had just cried, "Where are the Salish?"

"Are the people of this country so tormented that they cannot step forth from their lodges? Look at the grasses — these trails are overgrown! This is the Place of Trading, yet no man's foot has trod here since — " Abruptly he stooped to the grass that his foot had been sweeping to one side. When he straightened he held in his hand a broken-shafted arrow. It was a war arrow, with the stain of poison on its tip.

Holding the arrow in his hand he turned and looked at his people, who were still standing silently, staring at him, wordless and motionless, holding their packs.

"The chief of the march has given order to make camp. But you do not. Weary — you will not rest. Hungry — you will not eat. But take heart, people of my heart, for Running-Elk too knows that this valley feels like the haunted lodge of the dead."

Their shaman stepped forward. He was rawhide-lean,

a man of strange silences and habits, and even stranger speeches, though no man cared to contradict him. He held up a large, bone-thin hand of warning to Running-Elk.

"Speak not lightly here of ghosts and of haunting, Running-Elk, chief of the Spokans. Heard you not the sob of the echo that took up your question, 'Where are the Salish?'"

It is said among the Salish that after many years of self-discipline, and countless hours of isolation, their shaman can see and talk with ghosts. Normally, the spirits of the dead linger about their old haunts for no longer than four days and four nights, after which their footsteps can be found on the Milky Way, the shining path of stars that they have walked to that Great Happy Place where the air is always light and warm, and food is plentiful, and work is easy.

But Running-Elk knew that sometimes things can happen to upset the spirits of the dead so that they do not go their usual way. He saw several of his people reach for their charm bags. In these were the tokens of their guardian spirits, which, if strong enough, would keep the ghosts away.

The shaman had his eyes closed. His head was up, as though he were listening. Running-Elk, after giving him some time, asked quietly, "Do they wish us harm?"

For a time it seemed that the shaman had himself gone out into the spirit world, and could not hear. But after a moment he opened his eyes.

56

"They are timid, because we are strangers. They cannot hurt us. They are frightened, and they weep. Some of them are the ghosts of children."

At these words a soft sound of sympathy went up from the women:

"Lead them home, our shaman! Lead the little lost ones over the white sky trail, so that their tears may be dried, and their sobbing cease!"

But the shaman shook his head.

"Of myself, I cannot," he said, "for they are so young, they are used to the ways of women. They are timid, and will not come near me, because I am a man."

So it was decided that the people should go on, but that one woman, a mother, should stay behind and help the shaman make friends with the lost and bewildered spirits, so that he could guide them along their rightful path.

But women almost never take part in spirit dealings, which are reserved for those who have the strong medicine of the sun for their guardian spirit. So now they in turn were timid, and none would come forward to help the shaman.

The people all discussed the matter, their soft voices blending into a hum like the drone of the honeybees tumbling heavily through the grasses and the late-blooming lupine. After a while the sun went down, and the strangeness of the valley chilled their skin, and the women were even more afraid.

Then Bright-Star, wife of Standing-Bear and mother

of the young Nkwala, stepped forward, and she said:

"My son's growing-up ceremonies have run into many days and nights, yet in all his time spent alone Day Dawn has not permitted harm to come to him. For this I am grateful. Therefore I, Bright-Star, will have compassion upon the spirits of these children who have been less fortunate.

"I shall remain behind with our good shaman. I shall sit near where the little ghosts cry, and I shall move slowly, so that I may not frighten them. And I shall sing to them the songs that I sang to my son when he was a babe in my arms.

"And pray for me, all of you, before you sleep, for the heart of Bright-Star even now beats loudly and hard. Yet Bright-Star wishes to be brave.

"And lend me an empty cradle, one of you my friends, for it may be that the ghosts of the little ones will be drawn to a cradle as a birdling is drawn to the nest."

So it was that the Spokans did not linger in Soiyus, the Place of Trading, for which they had held such high hopes. They were driven on, as they had been driven now for days, by the feeling of treachery and tragedy that had filled the long valley.

Nkwala looked back on the Soiyus basin, which was filling with dusk. His mother's figure was small in the distance, and suddenly he found that he could go no farther. His feet refused to carry him. He would not leave her!

Just as he stiffened in defiance he heard his father's low voice behind him:

"And is the child of Bright-Star less brave than his mother? Rest easy, my son, we camp just yonder. And well it is that I can read my son's mind from the back of his head!"

Another fireless meal. Another night of sleeping with their moccasins on. Another camp hidden and guarded.

When all was quiet, Nkwala silently raised himself to his hands and knees. He was going back to watch over his mother. Peering, he leaned over his father to make sure that he was asleep. He was startled to find himself looking into Standing-Bear's wide-open eyes. The man nodded, and the two of them slipped silently out of the camp, doubling back on their trail at a fast trot.

When they could see and hear Bright-Star, they settled themselves comfortably and watched, and wondered if she were very frightened; for the shaman, there beside her, was swaying with strange, trancelike movements; and undoubtedly his spirit was walking the white path of the sky, and the motions of his body proved that up there his spirit was even now carrying some small thing tenderly and carefully in his arms.

True to her task, Bright-Star continued to sing the ancient lullabies and rock the empty cradle in her arms.

And the coyotes, sensitive to whatever sound they hear, echoed the loneliness and the long-ago quality in their singing. And the beautiful sound that means water is near —

the throbbing chorus of the frogs — added itself to the singing of the woman, the coyotes, the night birds, and the night winds.

Nkwala leaned back against his father's shoulder and looked up at the white sweep arching the sky.

"More footsteps are added to that trail this night," he murmured, "our shaman, and those whom he guides. And some far, far day, when the coyote howls over Nkwala's returning trail, he too will walk there. Perhaps it will be a a lovely night, like this one, on which my mother sings."

When the shaman's spirit had come back from its task, and completely returned to his body, the four of them went back to the camp.

III

THE BAT had not long gone to rest before the Spokans were eating their morning meal and making ready for the trail.

Presently the sky flushed a delicate pink, like pink phlox on a hillside, and the chief of the march cheered them on, saying, "Lend speed to your moccasins today, my friends, and it may be that tomorrow you shall draw the circles for your lodges!"

And to his scouts he said, "Listen for every sound, and watch for every sign. And when you hear no sound, and when you see no sign, remember that is the time of danger, and be careful indeed . . . be careful indeed!"

The people were thinned down. Their skin was dry from

the hardship of the journey. They missed the cleanliness of body that was such an important part of their daily life. But hearing the words of the chief of the march, their spirits rose at the thought of being able to sit again before their own lodge fires — fires that would mean hot brews to drink, and, most necessary for their strength, fresh meat to eat.

So they continued their swift journey north, giving up the nearness of the stream for the sake of the safety afforded by the base of the hills on the eastern side of the valley, and by the cover of the larger trees.

They traveled through rabbitbush and sagebrush and gold, dry grass, over boulders of forgotten riverbeds, and skirted tule rushes hiding the wet edges of a boggy marsh. They came upon sudden, unexpected little cups of lakes, with the shadow of great depth in their center; but all these things they saw only quickly, in passing.

The day was well spent and exhaustion was dragging at their footsteps when on the crest of a hill a scout appeared.

He gave the sign for attention, both hands raised high over his head, then swung apart, and again high. Then he turned sideways toward them so that they could better follow his motions, and drew his hands close to his chest, then swung them out in a circle before him, and back again, against his chest. Then, in the space of time no greater than the beat of a bird's wing, he had disappeared, and, on a hill that seemed to have no cover, no trace of life could be seen.

The chief of the march nodded his approval. Better scouting and signaling than that no tribe could boast!

"Lake," the signal had read, and when they saw the lake a cry of delight broke from their dust- and sun-parched lips. For here was no meadow-lake, as at Soiyus, but a great sweep, mountain-flanked.

Full, wide, and miles long, it stretched placidly before them, its rolling hills repeated in floating reflection, clear, perfect, and unbroken. The people ran to a sandy shore and thrust their arms hungrily into the water and splashed it on their faces.

Watching the longing of their reaching hands, their chief of the march decided to relax his stern discipline enough to permit a cooling swim.

But no Salish walks rudely and abruptly into a strange lake, any more than he would walk rudely and abruptly into a strange lodge. So great a lake must be duly complimented and praised for its beauty, for if the Spirits of the Lake were displeased with the people's conduct, they would punish them for their rudeness by causing them to become sick.

So their shaman, whose medicine was the strongest among them, stepped forward and gave the sign of good will and blessing to the shining water, saying:

"Hear these our words to you, O Lake, that we of the Spokans see you and call you great and bless you. For your kindness to us, we make you this gift of tobacco — thus!"

And he flung a handful of choice tobacco out upon the

lake's still surface. The fingerlings and minnows rose to investigate, and because the tobacco had grease mixed into it, they found it interesting and acceptable.

"We thank you, O Lake, for quenching our thirst, and for the sweetness of your cooling touch upon our bodies. Accept us kindly, O Lake, for this is our prayer to you."

Then the men and the boys went to one section of the little beach, and the women chose a section that was screened by a stand of dwarf maple, for modesty is a part of the great dignity of the Salish people.

Nkwala cut through the water like a golden-brown fish, for they were all trained from early childhood to be strong swimmers. In a matter of brief minutes, they were called out to dress and resume the march.

But now the lake was their marching companion, and although the flat trail had given way to climbing, and the way was often rocky, the lake was close and its cool breath was a gentle touch. Happy, too, was the fact that the end of their long journey was close before them.

Sunset was blazing across a blue mountain line when the chief of the scouts doubled back and greeted his superior, the chief of the march, thus:

"I, Fleet-Arrow, chief of the scouts, salute you and ask for a small time of talking and of council."

The chief of the march in turn summoned the head chief, Running-Elk, also Standing-Bear, the father of Nkwala, and all the senior men of the band. When they had gathered, the young scout spoke:

65

"This we your scouts have seen, and I come to tell you. Lakes we have seen on our journey; first small quiet lakes at the place of trading, then this great and friendly lake we walk beside. It received us, and we swam and were refreshed, and the lake knows us, and is kind.

"Now, just ahead, the land gathers this lake in to its ending, and beyond that land, which is many steps, there is yet another lake, and this strange water we go not near, for it is the Lake of the Monster.

"Over the crest of the hill before you, and beyond a sandy shore, is this Lake of the Monster; all this territory is the land of the people called Okanagon. The lake stretches farther than the eye can see, and is indeed of such beauty as we have heard spoken. Yet we go not near it, for fear of that mystery which lives within.

"It must be, therefore, that the land of the valley floor between these two lakes is of the name Penticton, 'the Place Where the Lake Is Gathered In.'

"Game we have seen, and the tracks of game without number. But of the people called Okanagon we have seen nothing, nor the fresh sign of these people. Some deserted lodges lie open to the rain, and silence fills them. There is quiet beyond our liking. That is all."

Then their chief scout sat down and leaned his back against a rock, for he was weary. For him and for his men the long trek had been doubly hard. But they took a fierce pride in the perfection of their work.

While listening, Running-Elk had been studying the

sky where cloud after cloud caught fire from the sinking sun.

Now he spoke.

"Of the Lake of the Okanagon we have heard. It is spoken of by all who travel far. It is moody and of a quick temper, for in its great depths lives Nhaw-hetq the Monster.

"Therefore I ask that you go not near this lake, any of you, until we of the Spokans have learned the right medicine and offered the right gifts. With the red paint of ceremony upon our faces, we shall speak in courtesy and offer our gifts. Until then, go not near.

"Walk in good conduct, each one of you, for it is to here we have come to escape from the long drought. Whatever waits in this country of good or evil for the Spokans, we meet it here."

Nkwala looked about him with his eyes shining.

"This is good!" he whispered to himself. "By the feel of my skin upon me, and the things I see with my eyes, I, Nkwala, behold these things and call them good!"

Then he sat down on his buckskin breechcloth with his heels tucked under him, and he tobogganed down the hill, so that, with his pack jogging crazily behind him, he was racing up and down the clean sandy shoreline of the friendly lake whose eastern side they had been following most of the day; the others arrived more slowly, having preferred to travel on their feet.

Seeing his son running up and down the shoreline Stand-

ing-Bear turned to the boy's mother, and said, "There, my woman, is your 'little spotted sandpiper'!"

Then they found they had to turn aside to hide the tender shared laughter that was bubbling up inside them, for it is considered unseemly in the Salish to make public display of emotion or family affection.

But Nkwala's high-spirited joyousness, his exuberant delight in the fragrant air, the rioting sunset, the softly rolling mountains, the clean, crunching, pale-gold sand, and the lake whose touch they already knew, made everyone lighthearted.

They hung their carrying bags and their packs on tree branches, and straightened and stretched from the weight of the burdens they had carried overlong.

The women found long forked sticks, and began gathering dead branches from the trees for firewood. The men took stone axes, and jade axes, and adzes, and wedges of antler from their packs, and the light dusk of the evening heard their hammer blows fall and the trees go down, to make their lodges. And when the waning moon gave them only half its face for light, they came in and made rough beds of fir branches over which they threw their robes.

But they lit no fire to tell of their coming. And though they slept the sleep of those who feel they have come home, yet their moccasins were upon their feet; their weapons lay ready at their finger tips; and all night long with the night sounds, the cries of their scouts signaled from hilltop to hilltop.

The morning came softly, and each family said its morning prayers. The chief chose the bathing place for the women and children, and that for the men and boys. Nkwala stepped dripping from his swim and began to rub himself down with the tender, sweet-smelling tips from fir branches.

Something rippled the waves of rushes beside him, as a fish ripples the surface of the water.

"A beaver?" he thought. "A turtle?" Even his skin listened, with the wild awareness of the wild.

The rushes moved again, with the thrust of weight against their base.

Nkwala leaped like a lynx, and in half a breath was standing facing the moving rushes with his bowstring drawn taut and the arrow keen for its singing flight.

Now the motion in the rushes was constant, and coming toward him. He stared at it more in puzzlement than fear, and watched its slow approach. The rustling ceased. Two eyes were staring at him fixedly — the sensitive lines of the head he knew on instant sight. A coyote! But what manner of thing was this — a coyote crawling on its belly and coming toward him with prayer in its eyes for whatever kindness was in the heart of man?

Would it leap? Was it mad?

Then it whined, and Nkwala's experienced hearing caught the difference that the rushes had concealed from him. This animal was a dog. But dogs can go mad too.

70

And surely an animal must be mad to behave as this one was doing!

He kept his arrow trained on the animal, while the dog, with a sort of desperate courage, and knowing full well the shafted death that hung above her, dragged herself over the sand, begging with her eyes, while the pointing tip of the arrow followed her every inch of the way.

When the animal's teeth were within slashing distance of his feet, Nkwala felt a tremor of fear pass over his body, but he did not move, except to follow her slowly with his arrow.

Then the animal laid her head upon Nkwala's bare foot. And when she was not struck, after a moment she sighed a great sigh, like a creature come home.

And Nkwala's bow and arrow fell to the sand as he went down on his knees and took the dog's head in his arms. She crawled onto his lap and buried her head under his arm, and they were still, the two of them.

Then, over the light sounds of the tiny wavelets and the soft breath of the air in the rushes, Nkwala heard another sigh, with something of the weight of responsibility burdening it.

He looked up in surprise and beheld his father with his bow at half draw. Instinctively he clutched the dog more tightly, protecting it against his father's arrow. But Standing-Bear smiled and shook his head.

"Nkwala's quarry is Nkwala's quarry, whether he wishes to kill it or hold it in his arms, and Standing-Bear

71

would not interfere. But — " and he gave the familiar gentle tug at Nkwala's hair knot — "the father claims the right to protect his son. And I did not know what the animal intended."

Nkwala ran his fingers through the animal's coat, which was poor and would need some combing, and he did not want to get up from comforting her. Standing-Bear reached into the little pouch sewn to his quiver, and took some strips of dried meat, which he gave to Nkwala, and the boy offered to the dog. Half starved though she was, she took them daintily.

"She has seen trouble!" cried Nkwala compassionately. "She has seen great trouble. And I . . . and I . . . What is this feeling within me?"

Standing-Bear's eyes were grave.

"It is strong medicine, my son. The animal has claimed you.

"It is said that in the days of the world's first morning, before even these mountains were born, only animals moved upon the earth. And these animals made ready the earth for man, giving him a debt that stands through all time.

"Maybe it is because of this debt — I cannot say for I do not know — but this I will tell you, for you will learn it, and not without pain:

"Once in a long time, a creature from the animal world lays claim against a man's heart. And that man's heart is never again as it was.

"I, Standing-Bear, have seen this thing happen once before. This is an ancient thing, my son. As ancient as blood, and as well trusted."

Then Nkwala dressed, and the two of them walked back to the busy camp, the tall, straight, proud man and the boy who was growing more like him every day. With every step, Nkwala felt the dog's touch against his legs.

The people looked at the dog, and said nothing. And because they said nothing, Standing-Bear's hand went to his son's shoulder.

Their chief, Running-Elk, did not pause in his work. But he read the silence, and he read Standing-Bear's gesture, and he pondered whether to bring this thing out into the open now, or let happen what would happen.

The warm brown eyes of Bright-Star too were studying this thing, and the feeling of the people reached her like waves running up a shoreline. These were her people, but this was her husband, and this other was her son. And when they approached with the strange dog pressing itself against her son's legs, she reached into her food basket and took dried meat, and offered it to the dog.

That told the people her mind.

Then the four of them, Standing-Bear, Bright-Star, Nkwala, and the strange, distrustful dog, stood silently facing the silent people, and Running-Elk saw that the the time had come for talk.

"Let my people speak of the thing that causes them to

set their faces against those of their own band," he ordered quietly.

The people were embarrassed, because Standing-Bear was one of their most valued men, and his pride was a thing none of them cared to cross. Finally one said:

"The thing that is in the mind must be spoken. Can Standing-Bear be our friend when the dog he is taking into his lodge brings us ill luck?"

"How say you this?"

"She is the leftover of a lodge of trouble. Does the hunter use the arrows of a dead man? Do the people walk in his moccasins? Do they eat his food? All these things are bad. So it is with the dog. She is from a dead lodge!"

The speaker, a man heavy with muscle, stood defiantly, his feet apart, his thumbs stuck into the belt of his breechcloth.

In sharp contrast, their lean shaman uncoiled himself with slow deliberation from where he had been sitting on the ground, and as slowly moved over to examine the dog. His every motion said, "Time . . . time. What have the Spokans to do with haste?"

The dog bristled and showed her teeth, but she submitted to his touch. After a moment, there were five, not four, facing the people, as the shaman straightened and said mildly, "Is the father of the speaker's father living?"

"No, shaman, he is not. He has walked The Path."

"Mine, too, has walked That Way, and my father after

him. We all come from dead lodges, and we bless them in our memory."

"The dog is part coyote!" said another, trying a different approach, for they were still afraid of a dead man's property.

That was true, but it was true of a good many of the dogs of the Salish. And it was known that the Okanagon dog, more than any other, hunted with its master.

"If she be coyote, she must be good indeed," replied Standing-Bear, quick to seize a point. "Your own words come back to you, in that you told Nkwala my son that the coyote would bring Nkwala luck. Can the coyote then hurt Nkwala's people?"

Running-Elk watched gravely. It was well if the thing were talked out. Sullen silence was the thing that made trouble.

Supple as a coil of hemp rope and almost the same color both in skin and clothing, the shaman seated himself again on the ground.

"The dog will speak," he said. "Wait quietly, and in a little time she will speak." He was studying the shadow of a young pine. A straight young pine, its shadow marking the hours true as a sundial on the gold sand.

No one contradicts a shaman. But after a time they grew restless.

"Why do we wait?"

The shaman turned so slowly it was a rebuke.

"For five days and five nights, since the finding of the

75

'enemy firewood,' we have waited — waited for someone unseen to strike with an unseen hand — as the signs show has been done before. Our enemy walks unchallenged through our dreams. And you say to me, 'Why do we wait?' "

There was silence. The dog felt the trouble and remained motionless, tightly pressed to Nkwala's side. The black shadow of the young pine swung on its slow axis with the passing minutes. The people barely moved. Their shaman had spoken.

Suddenly, in the silence, the dog went rigid. Her chaps, that outer flesh above her teeth, wrinkled and drew far back, laying bare the full fighting power, the unhindered slashing power, of savage jaws.

It was to Nkwala she had given her heart, and it was before Nkwala she placed herself now in near-silent fury. She was facing down a trail that dissolved in peacefully sleeping green shadows. The people stared at her in growing concern, for she was in fighting stance, with even her toes spread for every advantage the ground offered. Low in her throat she challenged the utter silence with a growl that sent chills down the backs of those who were nearest.

Now the people were nervous of attack and they too were watching the shadowed trail and tensing. Then the shaman gave a sharp, commanding hiss, and the dog went crazy. Had she been half killed she could hardly have felt it, for, with the shaman's order, she herself had become fighting rage.

76

To her mind she had been told to defend this boy human she had chosen, and a camp of three hundred strangely hostile people, against the enemy approaching through the shadows of the trail.

She obeyed.

So it was that the young Spokan night scouts, coming in high-spirited and hungry, racing each other in their silent buckskin moccasins, ran unwarned and unprepared into the fury of an animal that attacked them all four at once.

Being wise young men and in no mood for battle, they promptly took to the tree branches. From that point of safety they looked down with amazement upon the four-legged fury on the path.

This was too much for the people, whose nervous tension had suddenly left them. One great shout of laughter burst from them. Then the sight of their scouts hanging in the trees kept them shrieking with laughter till the tears ran down their faces.

The four young men enjoyed all the attention and clowned happily, for the Salish greatly love a joke.

As for the dog, she was thoroughly content in having treed the enemy, and ready to make friends with them when Nkwala asked her to. The people whose eyes had been so unfriendly now praised her, called her a keen-eared watchdog who would make their sleep more safe. She accepted their friendliness, but would not move from Nkwala's side.

The coming of the Spokans had brought the company

78

of birds that like the nearness of man. A great shaggy raven turned in the blue sky from the aerial acrobatics which had shaken off the crows that were chasing him. He settled boldly on a low branch in the center of the camp and studied the people, turning his triangular head to watch them. The man who had spoken against keeping the dog called for silence. Then he wove the raven, and the dog, and the lake into his speech, in the mystic and poetic manner of the Indians — for the raven is a symbol of wisdom:

"The people of the Spokan band are honored, for the Wise One visits them," he said, pointing to the big black bird. "He comes from the sky to tell us that we did not want the dog, but now we have the dog, and this thing is a good thing." He paused, and the people murmured their approval.

"The Wise One says that therefore this lake shall be called by the name of Dog: 'Skaha'!"

Someone picked up a stick and beat upon a tree trunk as though it were a ceremonial drum:

"*Tat, tat, tat-tat!*"

The shaman stepped forward, raised his arms in salutation and blessing to the lake, and said, "Skaha!"

IV

S O BY THEIR OWN NAMING it was to Skaha
Lake that the Spokans had come. It was on
the northeast shore of Skaha that they drew
the circles for their lodges with bark rope, and dug in the
clean, good earth, with freshly cut digging sticks.

As true as the position of the stars in the sky were the
positions of the four heavy supporting timbers of each
lodge. Northeast and southwest, and northwest and southeast.

No Salish lives or moves without full knowledge of direction.

80

Each big timber bled a little at being cut, and barked and taken from its forest.

Now the murmur of its branches would be replaced by the soft tones of Salish voices. Instead of birdsong, it would hear the warm muttering of the lodge fire. Never again would it bear the weight of the quiet snow, but it would hold a safe roof over Salish heads. No bird would seek it out at nesting time, but on it would hang the basket that held the comfort of a man's pipe and tobacco.

After the big uprights came the side rafters and horizontal poles, everything balanced, strengthened, and tied with willow withes; then the long narrow poles like split wood that made the roof. Over the roof were thick layers of pine needles, and finally, earth. And under Salish hands, the earth went on with its growing of green things. For where the Salish moves, the forest does not alter.

From the outside, each lodge was a big cone of earth, with a notched log leading, like a ladder, down into the center of its fragrant hollow.

A new ground house, sweet with the raw odor of living timber, perfumed with its carpet of evergreen needles, its flat slab of stone that was the home's hearth waiting for cooler days when the lodge fire would burn indoors unceasingly. The warm smoke would rise from the coned center, and the sound of laughter. The ladder would become worn with the pressure of moccasined feet. And each person going down into the busy depth of earth would give the smoke-hole cry "A'la!" to allow the women who were cooking time to protect the food from dust from above.

The man-plant would winter and thrive, safely rooted in the good earth.

But for now, though their lodges were completed and they reached for their fire sticks and their tinder, Running-Elk still shook his head and said, as he had been saying since their arrival, "We build no fire to tell the far hills of our coming, for we are not yet ready to greet what the far hills may hold."

And the people began to wonder when they would be ready. But Running-Elk was their chief, so they kept their silence.

Nkwala murmured a little, in the safety of his own family.

"My stomach hungers for fresh meat," he said to his mother when she gave him mixed pounded seeds and berries, and minced dry meat.

"Even my dog Running-Fawn ate of fresh hare this early morning."

Bright-Star gave him one of her gently reproving looks. "And did your dog, whom you call Running-Fawn, light a fire to cook her hare?"

But Standing-Bear did not take so light a view of his son's words.

"My son," he said gravely, "it is in the history of the Salish that whole bands have died of starvation. Our chief has led us safely and wisely, and there is game aplenty in this valley. It is not for us to complain, lest evil come upon us."

Then Nkwala went over and hid his face in his father's shoulder, as he did when he was unhappy or ashamed. But he had a young and eager stomach, and it was true that it felt its hunger keenly.

After the people had eaten, Running-Elk called them together, and he said:

"Now hear these my words, while I give you my reasons, for it is right that my reasons should be known to you.

"Winter lodges you have built today, which is a day in the heat of a hot summer, for, when the gray goose flies south and the days grow cool, the moon of the hunting and the time of the tanning of hides and the drying of meat will be upon us, and in those days will be no time for building. Therefore did we build today.

"And because it was said to you, 'Remember the torn lodges of this valley where an enemy has struck, and make each timber heavy,' that, too, you have done, and well; the men laboring with the women, and even these our children helping with the digging and the stamping of the earth. And it is good.

"But the easy path and the safe path are two paths. They walk different ways. Therefore Running-Elk asks his people if they still will tread the rough trail with him."

He paused, and the people, who were weary and had known neither full rest nor warm food since their long trek began, answered with one voice:

"Let Running-Elk and his council lead. We follow."

Then Running-Elk pointed to the high clay cliff that their lodges half circled. And he showed them the whole plan that was in his mind.

"See, people of the Spokans, our friends the bank swallows have shown us the way. Under their nests, high in the face of the cliff, we shall dig caves, and screen the front of the caves with branches. At all times there shall be a little food and water in the caves.

"This must be, for we have come at the time of warring raids and of spilled blood. We shall be blamed as killers. Because of this, until after a time of talking — if indeed they let us talk — there is no friend for the Spokans in all this country.

"The fire of battle brings with it the blinding smoke of hatred, and we the Spokans have walked into this smoke.

"It is yet another bad thing that, though we did not wish it so, we are come here unknown and without permission. This is a serious matter, for it breaks the ancient law, and turns men against us.

"We are strangers come upon a strangers' battleground, yet whoever looks upon us will believe he sees his foe, and will strike to kill.

"The hand is on the war knife.

"When we are attacked, if our sentries forewarn us, and if we have time, we shall reach the caves. If we have not time, then we have built our lodges of great strength to keep safe our women and children, and we shall fight from

the lodges as best we can. Is this thing good in your eyes? Running-Elk waits your answer!"

In every night wind the Spokans listened for the footfall of their enemy, knowing that sooner or later he must come. So they looked at the place for the caves, which would be a fortress, and they gave answer:

"This thing is good in our eyes!"

They picked up their digging sticks and followed their chief up the cliff face, and they passed the dug earth out in baskets, and smoothed the path of their ascent, and strengthened the caves with timbers, and screened the front with branches, and put in a little food and water.

When they had finished they looked like clay people, so covered were they with the fine clay dust a man could hardly recognize his companion. They leaned on their digging sticks, limp with exhaustion, and laughed at each other, joking, and saying, "Is this you? How do I know this is you when I cannot see you?"

Listening to them, Running-Elk smiled at their teasing, and the dust cracked in the laughter creases of his face.

"This great puzzle of who stands before you," he called, and his voice rang out over the camp, "can best be solved in the waters of the Lake Skaha!

"Hear me now — " He held up his hand and checked them, for the eager people had begun to race toward their bathing stations.

"While we worked at building a safe place and a battle

place in the cliffs, three of our hunters were sent upstream in the western ravine in the mountains. The shadows have lengthened to the east since their leaving. Soon the winds will bring us their signal to help carry in the game, for the guardian spirits of these men are the hunters' friends and they have found favor with our animal friends all the days of their hunting.

"Therefore, when you are bathed, look to the fire sticks and the tinder, and light the campfires of the Spokans! Let the red embers heat the cooking-stones, and let the gray smoke rise to tell the far hills and all who watch the skyline that here is a people that lights its fires in the open, and brings harm to no man.

"But let the gray smoke say to the sky, and let the far hills mark it well, that no enemy will stamp out the fire of the Spokans — and live!"

The men of the band answered their chief with one shout from their dust-parched throats. The next moment they were secluded at the water's edge, shaking great clouds of dust from their clothing, for in the ancient days vast clouds of volcanic ash had fallen over this country, and the dust of the white cliffs was fine and light. Then the people swam and splashed, while the sun caught the flung spray and turned it to tossed gold.

Running-Fawn, Nkwala's dog, was content with shaking herself thoroughly, thereby creating a small dust storm of her own, for she had been hunting moles in the cliff. Then she lay down by Nkwala's clothes to guard them.

Clean and bathed, the people worked the fire sticks until the teased bark caught the spark, and the first thin curl of smoke grew to a flame. The women laid out what few food mats and dishes they had been able to carry the long miles.

Presently the new camp welcomed its returning hunters. The meat that they would eat this evening had been quartered and chilled in a stream. The hunters and carriers as they neared camp were singing the mourning song for the death of the brown bear. This solemn chant was a necessary courtesy to the animal, an apology to its spirit, and a form of grace, or blessing, upon their food.

> *Brown Bear, Brown Friend, be comforted.*
> *Our feathered arrow whispered to your Shadow*
> *And said, "Come away,*
> *Come away, Shadow of the Brown Bear*
> *So that the People may eat the flesh and grow*
> *   strong."*
> *Brown Bear, Brown Friend, do not feel sad.*
> *Tell your friends not to feel sad.*
> *Your Shadow heard, and it went away.*
> *But it will come back, stronger than ever.*
> *We thank you for letting us kill you, Brown Bear.*
> *This is our Mourning Song, sung for you.*

The whole camp joined in the solemn singing. When the animal was skinned and the skull was properly cleaned, one of the young men was chosen to carry it up a hill and tie it into a tree, as close to the top as he could reach. There it stayed, in a place of honor and respect.

Nkwala wished that he were old enough to carry the bear's skull to a place of honor. Or the mule deer's proudly-antlered head, or the head of the big elk. But most he would like to carry the bear's head, for it was the one animal for which the mourning song was sung at its death. Also, the bear and the beaver were the two animals that knew best what people said, and what they were thinking. But a boastful hunter would be shunned by all animals. His stomach would go empty and his spirit would be humbled.

Soon the fat tender cuts were roasting on spits in front of the fires. Bark dishes caught the dripping fat. The delicious smell made the saliva form in Nkwala's mouth, and the keen desire in his stomach held the hint of pain, which was his body's way of telling him what food it required.

The Spokans ate with a great appetite. This was their staple food that kept their health and courage high and their mood calm. This was their strength. It was for this that they gave thanks in every prayer.

When they had finished, there was a little time for the courtesies that the Salish are taught to regard so highly. There were a few speeches, and a song or two. Each man felt his dignity restored now that a part of the earth was again his home, with its hearth and its doorway.

But the young man who had been wooing the maiden had no hearth of his own. As if to remind her of this, he sat with his flute outside the circle of the campfire, a lonely figure, playing the thin, sad woodwind notes that the shy young woman pretended not to hear.

And the little girls, of the age and size that little girls always are, turned their backs on their grownups and played at being mothers, as little girls always play; and poured out little-girl love to wooden dolls in buckskin dress with wooden, staring faces.

All these things were the return to normal, the restriking of roots. Nkwala felt his own problem rising again to the surface of his mind. He found that his thoughts were wandering from the speeches, and he peered through the evening mists wondering where he would find the mountaintop to renew his solitary night-searching for a guardian spirit.

Presently the dusk darkened to nightfall, and the deep bull tone of an old coyote signaled the pack to its singing. This was the wilderness answer to the Salish kill and the smell of blood on the night air. This was the "Good hunting!" from the wild and the free, this song that was picked up from lookouts and singing posts for five miles around, and rioted up to the stars. If the coyotes had killed early and were full-fed, they might sing all night. But if this night were for hunting, they would sing for a while, then quietly go their lonely ways.

Nkwala's dog whimpered for a moment as she felt the surging tug of her coyote blood. Then she settled down quietly, only her sensitive ears responding at times to the weirdly beautiful song.

"Nighthawk and coyote know the hour," the Salish would say, for when the coyotes gave voice, the nighthawk was cutting the sky into sharp lines of swift flight with its hunting on the wing.

While Nkwala was still thinking about his return to his growing-up ceremonies, he heard his father call. Standing-Bear put into his son's hands a beautifully carved pipe of polished brown soapstone.

"This my son will give to our shaman," said the man, "in return for the words and the wisdom that helped Nkwala to keep his dog when the people had turned against the dog."

Nkwala's eyes shone with excitement, for after the digging and the bathing, his father had taken time to find a piece of quartz crystal, and with it he had carved a picture of the sun — the shaman's emblem — upon the bowl. And below the bowl was a punctured flange, to which the shaman would tie the feathers of the golden eagle, as is a shaman's privilege. This was indeed a pipe for a shaman!

Nkwala carried it carefully, in both hands. And when he approached the shaman, the people hushed. The tall man rose graciously to receive the gift, and Nkwala was startled to hear his own voice sounding out over the camp. But this was as it should be, for one must speak clearly and slowly.

"I, Nkwala, son of Standing-Bear and Bright-Star, make this gift to the shaman of the Spokans, because he has spoken for Nkwala!"

A wordless murmur of approval rose from the Spokans, for the Salish are lovers of formality, and of well-chosen words, well spoken.

Then the shaman invited Nkwala to sit beside him, and that was indeed an honor for one so young. After a while the man of strange silences began talking to the boy:

"Mark this well in the mind of Nkwala, and write it deep — 'The things that are sure are the things that lie within reach.'

"Strong medicine is for the time of strong medicine, but when the people are angry or afraid, look you always to the little things that the people forget in their fear or their anger. For these are the things that can change the day.

"Our people, when they became angry today about the dog, forgot the appointed moment of their scouts' returning, even though this tree, this straight young pine, was marking the moment of the scouts' return with its black shadow on the sand.

"Remember the little things, Nkwala, and take time to use them."

Nkwala nodded, and put the shaman's words away back in his mind among the lessons that his life had taught him. But he had no dream of how soon and how desperately he would use that lesson.

V

THE NEXT DAY the camp of the Spokans took up its age-old pattern of life, but with this difference — that the women and the girls weaving the rush mats for food mats, and for wall mats, and for storage mats, were told to stay well within the camp and keep the children with them.

No berrying or root-digging party went out without an armed guard. And never a sentinel came in from guarding the camp but another first took his place. The Spokans were strangers in a strange land, and sooner or later their right to be in that land would be challenged.

Nevertheless, as each night came on, Nkwala begged to

be allowed to go out alone on his growing-up ceremonies, for he was feeling a fierce impatience with the time it was taking him to obtain his guardian spirit.

He pointed out to his father the mountaintop on which he wished to make his lonely vigil, and promised that he would not leave it, and would follow a straight trail there and back.

Standing-Bear and Bright-Star feared for their son, but they dared not refuse him, for the danger of spoiling the boy's courage. For his safety it was told to the scouts and the sentinels that the boy would go out on his ceremonies, and Standing-Bear pointed out to his son many times the exact path by which he was to go and return.

So once more Nkwala found himself trotting through darkness, carrying his bed roll, his water-basket, his bow and quiver of arrows. And although Standing-Bear could hardly have told why he had given it to one so young, Nkwala was carrying one of his father's best war knives. The boy lacked the muscle to use such a weapon. But its cool pressure against his skin inside his belted poncho was a constant reminder that he must keep to the shadows.

So it was not the open spaces, but the blotched, black-shadowed grounds of thick cover that heard the pebbles rattle in the ceremonial deer-hoof ornaments tied about his legs. His easy, springing trot put a rhythm into their sound, and the sound reminded him of his bad night — that night which was his secret and of which he never spoke, the night that fear had seized him.

He remembered the morning following that night, when, bruised and cut, he had stood alone on his mountaintop and raised his arms to Day Dawn, and shouted his vow:

"So long as Nkwala lives, Fear will never again have its way with him — *never!*"

And the echo of his vow had drifted back over the hills in the country of the Straight Water:

"Never! . . . Never! . . . Never!"

Presently he found himself again on a mountaintop, alone with the stars and the walking wind. He was near the Lake of the Monster — the long, long water of the Okanagon — but not too near, for the lake was not yet made friendly by their gifts and prayers.

Nor could he light his ceremonial fire, as it had not been considered safe for him to risk the attention that such a beacon might attract.

He was still weary from the march and the work following the march. The night lulled him comfortably. He stretched himself out on the bare ground.

His gaze went up, and up, and up, where the lights were faint as frost gleams in a "Forever" of space. He let his senses swim like a loosened bird in the terrible greatness of the night sky, till he felt that the pebbles and the earth under his back, his heels, the calves of his legs and the back of his head were pushing him upward, into the stars. And he thought, "Could a Salish boy fall *upward* in the night, as well as *downward?*"

96

And because there were stars up there that had once been people — for the old men told stories of them and pointed them out, in the sleepy storytelling hour, around the council fires at night — his fingers sought the earth and held to it like a comrade. Nkwala was an earth-child.

It was then that he heard the coyote.

When one can tell by a coyote's tracks whether he is playing or hunting, and by a coyote's voice whether he is singing or giving a message, one listens.

Nkwala listened.

Almost he gave answer. But with the breath for the call upon his lips, he paused. A vague uneasiness seeped through him like some dim discomfort he could not recognize.

Again the coyote's call — and Nkwala sprang to his feet with his body as cold as ice.

Though the years of Nkwala were to be long and his summers many, never was he to understand how his heart told him that his perfectly cadenced cry came from the throat of no coyote. This was a scout's signal, and a scout who could have come only by stealth, inside their own line of guard, where no scout should be!

The one spot they had left unguarded, the Lake of the Monster, had let their enemy through!

For that frozen second when his body refused to answer to his command, his mind pictured them, shadowy, the faint murmur of their voices, even the grating of canoes on the sandy shore.

And then he was running as he had never run before.

Faster even than on that night when fear had seized him and shaken him like a gopher.

But true to his vow, his mind, not fear, was his master now. His thought was for his people. He was calculating how soon he would reach the spot from which his warning cry could be heard in the camp.

What Nkwala could not know was that back in camp, when that first coyote call drifted in, so faintly against the wind that no Spokan heard it, his dog Running-Fawn set her ears sharply forward, got to her feet, and began running back and forth the length of her buckskin lead rope, whimpering in distress. She had been tied because she wanted to follow Nkwala.

Now the animal's strange behavior startled Bright-Star, who stared at the dog with widening eyes, while the rush mat she was weaving slipped unheeded from her fingers.

The way of an animal is the way of instinct. Bright-Star knew of the strong bond between this half-wild creature and her son, and she accepted the dog's actions as a sign that Nkwala was in trouble.

Standing-Bear saw his wife bury her face in her hands, moaning.

That night the thought of his son's lonely vigil had lain like a wound in the back of his mind. There had been no rest for him. He looked at the bent head and shoulders of his son's mother, swaying in the pain and torment of her anxiety.

Then the arrows his hand reached for were his war arrows, and the knife he grasped was his war knife, and he left the camp with a speed like the speed of the wind with only one thought in his mind — to find his son, safe.

Word passed swiftly of the man's leaving, and the talking and the laughter faded from the night. One woman rose and went into Bright-Star's lodge, and sat beside her stroking her hair, because she could think of nothing else to do to comfort her.

So it was that when father and son approached each other in the shadows, each wondered at the sound of the other's speed.

"The enemy!" gasped Nkwala. His father spoke no word but grasped his hand. Then it seemed to the boy that he had never run in his life before. They took to the open ground where the path was the clearest. When a deadfall lay in their way, the grip of his father's hand tightened and the man leaped like a mountain cat. To Nkwala, it was eagle flight, with the wind in his ears.

When they were within hailing distance of the camp a great warning shout burst from Standing-Bear, as great a shout as a deep-chested man can give. Seconds later, when they reached the camp's enclosure, they were in a scene of flight and confusion.

The Spokans knew that they were to reach their fort in the cliff face, and many were already there. But many

others had been working or sleeping in their lodges, and for those who had little children it meant several trips up the lodge ladders. Some of the older people, stiff from the long trip and hard work, were slowed in their motions.

They needed time. Only a little, but that little they needed desperately.

Suddenly, in the heart of this whirling storm of action, Nkwala felt calm and quiet come over him. His mother had seized him by the shoulders and looked him over to see that he was unhurt. Then, true to her nature, she had turned to helping others to reach the fort. Standing-Bear too was giving a hand wherever it was needed. Surely these two had passed on to their son, in his very blood stream, the urge to think first of his people.

And Nkwala *was* thinking of his people. He was thinking of their chief, Running-Elk, on that hot night when they two had leaned against a great boulder, when from the burden of his anxiety the man had repeated, over and over, the words, "No blood must flow!"

And he was thinking of the words the shaman had spoken to him, quietly, slowly, so that each word would make its mark in his mind:

"Remember the little things, Nkwala, and take time to use them."

And the words of his father:

"This 'safety' place I have not found. Does my son's heart yearn for such a place?"

In the fort he, Nkwala, might be safe. The fort was built

101

for safety, and there were strong men to guard it. But . . .

"Nkwala is one with his people," he had said.

And now not all of his people could reach the fort in time. Not though even now they were crowding the path toward it.

He remembered the shaman's words, "Since the finding of the 'enemy firewood' we have waited — "

Back on the trail that Nkwala and his father had covered, one single cry of hot blood and hatred cut the night winds.

The waiting was ended.

Standing-Bear's warning shout must have let them know they had been discovered, for they were giving voice upon the warpath.

Nkwala felt his fear, but he felt it strangely apart from him, as he acted upon his plan. He threw branches that were heavy with pitch upon the fire, and armloads of dry twigs. So fed, the Spokan council fire leaped high and hungry, flinging its flames and lighting the open space about it.

Then, further to draw attention toward himself and away from his fleeing people, Nkwala leaped with the flames, flinging his arms and shouting.

The startled stillness heard the words that formed unconsciously upon his lips, for this, at long last, was the Song of Nkwala for which he had searched during long and lonely nights. And this was the dance of Nkwala. They came to him, strong and whole, and without his searching, for Nkwala had at last found his guardian spirit, which was the courage within his heart.

And Day Dawn, the god to whom all children pray, watched from the high stars of the night sky.

The warriors of the Okanagon entered the Spokan camp running silently and swiftly, like the gray wolves of the north to the kill.

The singing, and the light of the flames, drew them. They did not see or hear the last of the Spokans hurrying up the path to the fort in the cliff face.

All they saw was a deserted camp with its council fire burning hot and high, and a young boy, dancing and singing like a thing gone mad.

They hesitated. Then they moved forward, and one of them caught the boy by the shoulder and flung him to the ground.

When Nkwala rose silently to his feet he faced the hatred that calls for blood. Instinctively his eyes sought the man who would be their chief. To him he made the sign of greeting, or good will. And though some small flicker of change passed over the man's face, a lesser warrior stepped forward and flung Nkwala again to the ground.

"The score!" cried an Okanagon. "Count the score, and kill!"

Somewhere a knife was lifted. But the Okanagon chief did not move, and he was not a man to permit others to

move ahead of him. He was puzzled, and he wanted to understand before he decided upon any action.

When Nkwala was flung to the ground for a second time his lowered line of vision caught a swift motion at the edge of the camp.

The Spokan scouts were in!

Some sound or warning had reached them at their lonely sentinel posts, and by relayed signals they had called each other in. Now in the black shadows beyond the firelight they were fanning out in formation behind the enemy's back.

One arrow, one life, and the "time for talking" would be lost forever. Nkwala screamed through the dust which the second fall had forced into his mouth:

"Running-Elk says no blood must flow!"

He choked, spat dust and sand, and called again:

"Running-Elk says no blood must flow!"

The shadows were silent. But the shadows were watching. Just watching, to see that no harm came to their own.

Some of the Okanagon were picking up the scattered robes and cloaks of the Spokans, and exclaiming with satisfaction over their richness and their workmanship, for the Okanagon, too, were proud and well-dressed. But others, more cautious, were looking about them, and listening. They heard nothing and saw nothing. The night held its secrets.

"This is not our way of battle," said one, uneasily. "We of the Okanagon fight openly, in hand-to-hand struggle.

But always these wicked ones have sneaked, struck, and run. This time they have left behind them one of their young. Let us kill him and leave."

"My people are not your enemy," said Nkwala, rising slowly, because he was bruised, and because he did not want his deer-hoof rattles to sound.

"Hah! The boy is impudent, and he lies!" replied the Okanagon. But their chief held up his hand.

"Wait . . . Hear you the boy's speech? Old winds stir the ancient echoes, and memory feels what it cannot name."

"Wait?" cried another, his voice shaking. "Did they wait to kill? One, my wife — and another, my child! I say kill! Kill and go!"

In the deserted lodge of Standing-Bear, Running-Fawn, forgotten, had settled down with coyote wisdom to chew through her buckskin lead rope. A final tug freed her, and with the wet chewed end dragging from her halter she leaped from the lodge toward where she had heard Nkwala's voice. She leaped joyfully against Nkwala and rubbed herself against his legs, but showed toward the newcomers not any of the bristling caution that was her way of meeting strangers. The man who had last called for killing lifted his hand and pointed.

"That is my brother's dog!" he cried hoarsely. "Do we still wait to kill?"

"Call her," ordered the chief.

He called, and Running-Fawn went obediently halfway

to the man, then abruptly turned and went back to Nkwala.

"I see you, I salute you, I know you," her manner said politely. "But this boy-human I have chosen as my own, and my concern is for him alone."

"I too know the dog," said the chief, "and it is in my mind that this dog would not make friends with those she had seen kill her master."

The younger Okanagon passed his hand wearily over his eyes, for he had been sick these many days with grief. But his mind was a fair mind, so he shook his head. Then in a tired voice he said, "I do not know."

But others too had suffered in the raids that had brought the sound of weeping to the valley, and they were less patient.

"The hunting territories of the Okanagon have been invaded," they said, pointing with a sweep of the arm to the strange lodges. "No man has asked our leave, and the old law stands. Death to the invader!"

"Death has been in haste and full-fed in the land of the Okanagon long enough," said the chief curtly. "Now Death can wait."

It is not the manner of any chief to override his council, and an angry cry went up from his men.

But the Okanagon chief put Nkwala on the other side of himself, away from the strong-willed warriors, as he looked at them all levelly and said, "The boy is mine, for my lodge. I shall keep him."

He tilted Nkwala's face upward with a hand under his chin, and demanded sternly, "Speak words that are true, boy. From what place came you?"

"Southeast by many days' walk," replied Nkwala, running his tongue over his lips, for his mouth had gone dry with horror at the thought of leaving his parents and his people. He knew the laws of pacts between tribes. Even in peace, if he were demanded, he must go.

In the terrible homesickness that swept over him he added, "By the Straight Water, and the still lake that — " his voice almost broke — "Nkwala has made his promise to that lake that he will return."

"There are lakes in this country," replied the Okanagon, not unkindly, but in a tone that said the matter was closed.

Not even Running-Elk could help Nkwala in this, though even now, with the women and children placed back and out of danger and his men armed and in fighting position in the fort, Running-Elk's voice sounded out over the clearing like a voice from the clouds.

"Running-Elk, chief of the Spokans, greets the chief of the people of the Lake of the Monster, and asks for talk."

No muscle moved on the face of an Okanagon to betray astonishment. Their eyes swept the cliff, which in the darkness revealed nothing.

"Let Running-Elk speak," replied the Okanagon chief. But from his men's throats rose again the angry mutter:

"The score, count the score! We are unavenged!"

"For miles to the south the signs lie bare," said the voice from the cliff, "and Running-Elk knows of your suffering. Therefore he asks that no quick move be made in anger while we talk."

"Running-Elk is the intruder," replied the Okanagon. "By what right does he ask so much?"

"The right of a friend. Stand safely, and judge if he would do you harm!"

With those words came the whistle of a war arrow with the force that could crest a hilltop. Seven feet above the head of the Okanagon it bit into the trunk of a pine, and the tree shuddered to its top branches.

"Stand safely yet again, and listen," said Running-Elk, for he, too, had seen his scouts move in and fan out behind the backs of the Okanagon. He gave three short, sharp coyote yips. Again there rose the coyote cry that came from the throat of no coyote, as the Spokan scouts answered their chief from the shadows.

"Talk, then, and we shall decide," replied the Okanagon. Not even for their lives would they admit that they had stepped into a trap.

"Have you one among you who knows the faces of your enemy?"

"Two warriors have seen the faces they will not forget!"

"Send them up with a torch from the fire, that they may look into our faces."

Accordingly two men moved forward, carrying light, setting the black shadows into writhing, twisting motion about them as they walked.

They were met by a young unarmed Spokan and guided up the path and into the fort. There they walked the path that opened for them as they moved, shining the light into one face after another. To the women and children they gave only the briefest glance, but they studied the men closely. They betrayed no flicker of interest in the number of warriors or the strength of the fort, but no detail of it missed their eyes. Then, as silently as the shadows that moved about them, they turned, went down the path, and back to their chief.

"These are different," they told their chief. "In all things these people are different. Our enemy fouls where he walks, like the wolverine. But these are clean and quiet, and they build where they come. They are a different people, and they are many."

"But by what right?" demanded the Okanagon of their chief. "By what right have these strangers invaded the hunting territory, and the root-digging grounds, and the salmon-stations of the Okanagon?"

Their chief and spokesman turned again toward the voice from the cliff, and he said:

"Why do the strangers choose to invade the territorial property of the Okanagon?"

This was a curt question, in that he did not address Running-Elk by name. Therefore Running-Elk replied as shortly:

"Are we grasshoppers, to die in the winter? And who speaks of choosing? The hills choose the path of the waters, and even thus our path lies beneath our feet, and we must walk it."

Then less angrily he added, "Drought scorched our lands. And over the roofs of our lodges hunger howled like an empty-bellied wolf standing over dried bones."

"Yet Running-Elk knows the law," said the Okanagon, "that the man who invades another's tribal territory does so under sentence of death!"

Now this was the moment toward which Running-Elk had been slowly and carefully working, and the very trees hushed their murmur for his words:

"Chief of the Okanagon, there is yet an older law, the Law of Amotqen, that a man may not spill his brother's blood — *for it is his own!*

"And I, O chief, I, Running-Elk of the Spokans, even now as I speak, make the ancient claim upon you, and upon your people. I claim — our blood right!

"In the name of the tribe that fathered both the Okanagon and the Spokans, the ancient Flathead Tribe, I lay claim for myself, and for my people, to the hunting grounds, and the digging grounds, and the berrying grounds, and the salmon-stations of the Okanagon. And further, O chief, when the drought has left our own land by the Ntoxetk, its hunting and its lodges are open to the Okanagon."

In the stunned silence only the waves on the shore

111

whispered, as they rose, and sank, and rose, and sank again.

Finally the Okanagon spoke quietly to his men, whose shocked faces he had been studying:

"It was of this I wondered when I heard the manner of the boy's speech. This is a big thing, a very big thing! What is my people's wish?"

The men replied, "Our haste was wrong. Now let our chief speak words of his own choosing."

The Okanagon again faced the cliffs, and introduced himself formally to the Spokans. Then he drove his bargain:

"I, Big-Star, chief of the Okanagon, give greeting to the Spokans, our blood-brothers from the Straight Water, and welcome them, and grant their rights throughout our whole territories. We shall be of one blood, Spokans and Okanagon.

"And this I ask to seal the pact: that Running-Elk give to Big-Star, for his lodge, the young one — this boy who danced and sang as the Okanagon entered the Spokan camp. This one shall be my son."

The price was high, but it bought safety for the Spokan people; therefore Running-Elk hesitated but a moment before he said:

"It shall be as Big-Star wishes. The boy, Nkwala, shall be his son. And now our women will prepare food for our brothers, the Okanagon."

Nkwala clutched his dog to his breast, and told himself that he was now a man, and would not cry. But, locked tightly in his arms, Running-Fawn heard the secret sobbing of his heart, and whimpered, and licked his face.

VI

FOOD was not wanting for the hospitality of Spokan toward Okanagon. Dried salmon they had brought aplenty for trade. Already the stone-lined ovens were cooling, in which great quantities of black moss, camas root and wild onions had been cooking for two days. Deer fat from storage and fat from the last kill were added. Fresh meat was taken from the smoke racks. The women and children had gathered pine nutlets and berries in quantity. And the tule food mats were new, upon which all this wealth of supply was being spread.

Pride in their work mingled with haste in the women's

114

preparations, while the Spokan men, smoking with their guests in well-earned leisure, watched and were well pleased.

But in all this activity neither Standing-Bear nor Bright-Star was seen. They had withdrawn, for it was not seemly that grief should be shown over a gift to the Okanagon chief. Not even the gift of a son.

As for Nkwala, he kept his eyes upon the ground. He was afraid to scan the people in search of his parents, for fear that, seeing them, he could not restrain himself from crying out.

The Spokans all felt the separation, but they dared not show pity to the boy, for this was a tribal matter.

It was not long before the hot meal was set out on the mats. With his arms outstretched, Running-Elk spoke blessing over the food prepared, and then they ate.

After the meal, when a relaxed and friendly spirit lay pleasantly over the camp, the shaman of the Spokan people asked permission to tell a story. His slow deliberation and quiet dignity impressed the visitors even before he began, and he began strangely.

"A ghost," he said, "is the pale color of a waning moon in a daylight sky."

The faces of the Okanagon sobered instantly. With ghosts and death they were far too well acquainted since the treacherous killing raids had begun against them in their valley.

Then, as abruptly, the shaman veered away from the

115

subject, and began the story of the Spokans. He told of how the Spokans had dreaded leaving their own territory, but of how the drought had finally forced them out. He told of their long trip to reach the valley, and how, when they reached it, the trail they followed showed signs of treachery and bloodshed. He told of their anxiety to reach the valley of Soiyus, the Place of Trading, so that they might spread word that their coming was in peace.

Then, with understanding, and with great sympathy, he told of what the Spokans had found at Osoyoos. He told of the troubled spirits of those who had lost their lives there. While he spoke, several of the Okanagon covered their eyes with their hands, for they had been off guard and their losses in life had been heavy at the "Gathered Together" or "Meeting Place."

The shaman told of the little ghosts, that could not find their way, who cried like the night birds in their loneliness, and of the spirits of those who were older, and of those who were in between; he said, "Even such a one as Nkwala, here, in size and standing."

From a swift glance the shaman saw the Okanagon chief wince. So it was as he had guessed: Nkwala was to replace a son of the same age who had died in the Osoyoos raid. The story went on, while his listeners scarcely moved.

He told of how the tiny spirits would not come to him, being afraid of him because he was a man. Then his voice softened till it was a thing of beauty to the listening ear, as he told of the gentleness and the courage of one woman;

116

and the tender lullabies she sang, and the empty cradle she rocked, till the frightened littlest ones came to her, drawn by her motherhood. Then he, the shaman, had taken them gently from her, and carried them as he guided the others, over the white path in the sky.

When he had finished speaking there was a long silence. For strong and proud men though they were, the Okanagon could not speak when their hearts were filled to choking.

Finally Big-Star, the Okanagon chief, said, "Bring this woman before us, that we may look upon her, and know such a woman."

Then the shaman stepped back into the shadows, and took Bright-Star by the hand, and led her forward. The Okanagon looked upon her, and they saw a gentle woman, a beautiful woman, with ermine and seashells wound in her hair — and her eyes were swollen with weeping.

After a long moment of study the Okanagon chief asked, "Why does the woman weep?"

But already his heart had sunk within him, for he knew why the woman wept. Very gently, the shaman made answer.

"Big-Star, chief of the Okanagon, this woman is the mother of Nkwala."

Slowly, as though he were utterly weary, the chief of the Okanagon rose to his feet. For a moment he stood, motionless and silent. The high, hot light of the campfire caught the silver wings of a moth, and the insect fell like

117

a falling star. The man shook himself free of his memories and spoke to the silent people sitting on the ground about him.

"Running-Elk, chief of the Spokan band, and you, the Spokan people, hear these my words to you.

"It is in my mind that the Spokans have come, unknowing, to where they were needed. And they have done, unknowing, that which should be done. Because of these things, there stands a great debt against the Okanagon.

"I, Big-Star, for myself and for my people, now in this place and in this hour, make payment of that debt. To the Spokan people, and to this woman who weeps, I, Big-Star of the Okanagon, give my only son."

Then he turned, took Nkwala by the hand, and led him to his mother.

Instantly such a shout burst from the Spokans as startled the sleeping hills. The men of the band leaped to their feet and surged forward, and not one was content until he had placed both hands upon Big-Star's shoulders, and in each touch the Okanagon felt the hand of a brother. His weariness fell from him and his face lit with happiness, for the comradeship of man for man is strong, and it is deep.

Then Standing-Bear, father of Nkwala, called for silence over the talking and the laughter, and he said:

"This night I, Standing-Bear, have seen great things, and the greatest of these is kindness. Big-Star has gladdened the lodge of Standing-Bear with the return of

118

Nkwala. Therefore his troubles shall be my troubles, and his gladness shall be my gladness. And further, hear me, his enemies shall be my enemies!"

Again the Spokan shout — and the echoes of ancient war drums began to throb in each man's veins.

Then Running-Elk, the Spokan chief, stepped for-ward:

"Never has Running-Elk, chief of the Spokans, led his people into war, and no love has he for the scalp dance. For when the warrior falls, the hunter lies dead. Then who kills meat for the lodge?

"Already the seed heads in the grasses are heavy, and we have missed the first-nose of the ascending salmon. The harvest days shorten and press hard.

"Yet the evil that struck this valley was not the way of warriors, and it was dark indeed, for it planned to leave no spark to say that once among these hills a lodge fire burned!

"Therefore let a chosen few of the Okanagon, and of the Spokans, go forth in search of these wicked ones who strike, and run, and stay hidden. Let our men carry the message, that it may spread.

"Send word to the enemy and let it reach him well, who-ever and wherever he may be. Send word by the smoke signal, and by the moccasin trail. Flash it with fire from the hilltops, and send it by runner to the lodges.

"Say that seven times the evil ones have struck in the valley of the Okanagon, and the eighth time is waited.

119

"Bid them haste, but with this small matter in mind, that as they have not behaved as men, so they shall not be treated as men.

"And then, tell them this . . . tell them that Salish stands with Salish, and the ancient fires are lighted.

"Tell them their welcome waits."

Thus Running-Elk ended his words. But it was told in later years, among the Shuswap, the Kutenai, the Stuix, the Wenatchi, the Yakima, and the Kalispel that the words of Running-Elk swept the country from the high timberlines to the shore of the Big Water. And it was told that the wicked ones ran away, and were never seen again.

But for now there was happiness to attend to, for this night Nkwala had found his guardian spirit, and, from this night on, he was no longer a child, but a "young person," a "young man."

The Spokan shaman brought out his own face paints, and he painted the red flame of courage, and the bright flame of the council fire, upon the forehead of Nkwala. For these two, he said, were the boy's guardian spirits.

Standing-Bear lifted the hemp headband from his son's head, and gave one last, gentle tug to the knot of hair that would never again be worn as it had been.

While all this, and more, was going on, the beating of a festival drum began, and the men put aside their pipes, as their deep voices took up the familiar songs of love and bravery. The coyotes joined in the singing, and the song

120

of the camp and the song of the hills joined in the night air to float out over the Okanagon valley until it spilled over the skyline.

❀

This is the Song of Nkwala which came to him as he leaped and chanted about the flaming council fire, drawing the enemy toward himself, and away from his fleeing people:

I, Nkwala of the Salish,
Cry the Song of the Leaping Flame,
How I rushed to tell my people
When the Okanagon came.

The high flame, The bright flame,
The full-fed Spokan council flame,
By its light I found my guardian,
Now in fire I trace my name!

I asked of the lonely hilltops,
But the far hills answered back,
"Nkwala, study the eagle's flight,
Study the coyote's track."

Now ends the lonely searching,
My people, the hours were long!
See me — I am Nkwala-grown!
Hear me — this is my Song!

GLOSSARY

Amotqen A great and good chief, source of life, lives in the upper world and rules it.

Cluster Stars The Pleiades. The Indians used to tell the time of night by them.

Day Dawn The children's god having especial care over them.

Enemy Firewood Bark of the Western Yellow Pine. Three long pine needles to a sheaf is positive proof.

Flathead The Flathead group consists of the Spokan and three other tribes. It is fairly widely assumed that they were so called because they wore their hair smooth and natural on top.

Giants In Nkwala's time, giants were believed to be common. They would crawl up to a tent or lodge and look down the smoke hole. They lived in caves in the rocks and had a

123

great liking for fish — often stealing them out of people's traps. Otherwise they did not bother people much.

Grizzly Bear Stars   The Big Dipper. Legend had it that the four stars of the bowl were the bear's feet — in other words, the bear itself. The three stars in the handle of the Dipper were hunters. Look closely and you will see a tiny star with one of the "hunters" — that is his dog.

Hemp   The long inner strands of bark, usually cedar, from which the Indians make ropes, sashes, headbands, etc. Also a plant.

Kinnikinnick   A smoking mixture. The Indians mixed bearberry leaves with a wild tobacco.

Little People   Dwarfs. They were fond of playing tricks, but they never kept any of the articles they had taken, and never killed or hurt people.

"My Spirit walked the white trail in the sky"   Fainting. The Indians believed the spirit left the body.

Nhaw-hetq   The Okanagon word for "monster" or "mystery." People today call that creature of Okanagon Lake "Ogopogo," and many claim to have seen it. The Indians used to make offerings to this same "mystery."

Ntoxetk   "Straight (or Smooth) Water." The Co-

	lumbia River below the Arrow Lakes, in the United States.
Okanagon	A tribe of the Salish. This is the Smithsonian spelling of the name. Other common spellings are Okanagan and Okanogan.
Penticton	Headquarters of the Penticton Band of the Okanagon-Salish Indians. The name means "Where the Lake Is Gathered In." The city of Penticton is at the south end of Okanagon Lake.
Peské pts	The spring season.
Salish	A nation of several tribes, including the Okanagon, Flathead, Spokan.
Slow match	A wrapped stick of cedar bark shreds. Some could keep a fire for over two days.
Soiyus	"The Meeting Place" — the Indian name for Osoyoos, a town two miles above the American-Canadian border, on the Okanagon River chain. It is still called Soiyus by the Indians and old-timers.
Tule	Cattail; bulrush.
Venison	Deer meat.
White Trail in the Sky	The Milky Way, believed to be the trail the spirits walked to their new home. The stars in it are their footsteps.